All That Remains

A Post-Apocalyptic EMP Survival Thriller

JACK HUNT

DIRECT RESPONSE PUBLISHING

Also By Jack Hunt

The Renegades
The Renegades 2: Aftermath
The Renegades 3: Fortress
The Renegades 4: Colony
The Renegades 5: United
Mavericks: Hunters Moon
Killing Time
State of Panic
State of Shock
State of Decay
Defiant
Phobia
Anxiety
Strain
Blackout
Darkest Hour
Final Impact
And Many More…

Dedication

For my family.

Prologue

The tempest raged.

Landon Gray felt the snow long before he saw it. The wind tore through the gaping hole, stabbing his body with cold. It thrust snow at his face with such force that it stung like tiny ice needles. He gasped, a futile attempt to breathe. How long was he out? Disorientation overwhelmed him. It was still dark. Was he up or down? More snow spilled in through the windshield, a wall of white before his eyes. Terror gripped him at the sudden sense of his mortality. Regrets; everything he hadn't done besieged his mind. Gale force winds shook the metal causing it to groan and sway.

He shivered and faded in and out of consciousness. The hazy pain brought him back. He blinked ice crystals out of his eyes. Was this how it would end? He tried to move, but a bolt of excruciating pain shot up his legs. Unable to catch his breath, he thought he would pass out again from the pain coming from his legs, or broken ribs? The thought of a rib collapsing his lungs and suffocating overwhelmed him. The taste of iron on his lips. Had he cracked his head open?

Another blast of wind, strong, steady and unforgiving.

Where was he? A momentary lapse as his mind tried to piece together what was a real or a nightmare. *The plane!* That was it. *Oh God.* More noise. Birds squawking, a wild animal roaring? More pain buried below indistinguishable sounds. *Smoke.* He could smell gas. *Fire.* No, no. He didn't want to burn alive. He opened his mouth to cry for help but a throatful of snow choked him. He coughed and spluttered, thrashing in agony, trapped by something heavy pressing down on his lower legs. His mind went hazy. Another wave of darkness. Complete nothingness, then gone, nothing but a blur only to be slapped awake by the chill of frigid air.

An acidic taste, followed by nausea, he wanted to throw up.

No, I'm not dying here. A primal urge to survive rose inside.

Landon clawed at his jacket, trying to find the keys; the keys with the small flashlight. The same one gifted to him by his son. His fingers sank into snow, the tips. Wet. Cold. Too cold. C'mon, you're not gonna die here, he told himself. More pain. Every movement invoked a torturous wave of agony worse than the last. He fumbled, clawing at fabric until two fingers touched metal and he heard a jangle. *Yes. Yes. Thank you, God.* He fished them out and clicked a button on the tiny flashlight, a strobe of bright light burst forth, slicing through the darkness like a laser. Shadows formed, dancing and flicking, revealing carnage, debris and disarray, then landing on the pilot.

Dustin. No. A large jagged tree branch had lanced straight through him pinning him to his seat. His face was gray and expressionless. If anyone should have survived, it was him. Dustin's voice came back to him as did the memory of treetops slapping beneath the fuselage before wings clipped then snapped branches. Would he die out here? *Help! A* croaky voice, barely audible, escaped his blue lips but was quickly smothered and hushed by the wind.

Another fragment of memory solidified in his mind.

They had to be at a high elevation as they'd traversed the Great Smoky Mountains over North Carolina before banking to the right. Dustin had wrestled with the plane, trying so hard to control the landing. *Brace for impact.* His final words echoed in his mind. A sudden drop, the feeling of free falling, faster and faster. Wind lashed at the wings sounding like maniacal laughter. Landon opened his eyes, not wanting to relive another second, it was too much. He angled the flashlight beam at the control panel. Unlit. No power. Covered in white.

Hello? Hello? Anyone?

He was alone.

Then like a spark, it came to him.

Ellie. As if his mind had blacked it out. His daughter was here with him. Fourteen. Spunky. Long flowing dark hair. Green eyes like her mother. *Where are you?* He twisted in the vise of pain, every inch hurting him more.

"Ellie? Ellie! Speak to me… Ellie! C'mon, baby."

Behind him, the seats that had once been there were gone, missing as well was the tail of the fuselage. His eyes scanned the darkness, the beam sweeping from left to right like a lighthouse.

Where are you?

Where are you!

Fear gripped him. "Ellie!"

Gone. A grief more powerful than the pain in his legs swallowed him.

Shivering, he tugged at his legs trying to free them only to wail in agony.

A flash of memory. Ellie smiling as they discussed how

they would spend Christmas, then lights blinked out, the plane surged forward into a nosedive and Dustin cursed as they entered a world of black far below. No city lights. No headlights. Nothing but pure darkness for miles in every direction. How? Impossible.

Ellie! Frantically he shone the light over snowdrifts. It bounced off pine trunks. He couldn't tell if the plane was off the ground or if pine trees and massive amounts of snow were supporting the jagged tube of metal. The light hit on something. A dark mound in deep snow. A trail of blood leading up to it. A seat. A face. Eyes closed, face drained of blood, a body contorted. An arm twisted in an ungodly position. Broken. Her leg angled backwards, the other hidden by snow... he began to breathe harder, darkness creeping in at his eyes as more snow blew and swirled around him.

The cold sucking the remaining life from his skin.

Struggling to control his gasping breath and pounding heart, he reached out calling her name but his voice was lost in the brutal wind. "Ellie..."

He blinked. She was gone. Nothing but snow for as far as the eye could see.

Was he hallucinating? Was his mind fabricating the worst outcome?

He wanted her so badly to be alive.

A glimmer of silver.

Something shiny in the snow.

The gifts. For Sara. For Max. For you, Ellie.

Groans of grief turned to wails. He cried so hard he choked on his tears.

It wouldn't be long and he would join her. He'd freeze to death before anyone came. It would all be over really soon. *Ellie… I'm sorry. I should have never brought you. I should have listened to your mother. I shouldn't have let you convince me. But you so desperately wanted to go. Please. Please. Be alive. I can't lose you.*

Landon shifted in his seat, pain stabbing his leg like a red-hot poker.

Stay with me.

His eyes closed.

Chapter 1

One day earlier

There was only one thing Landon Gray hated more than Christmas parties, and that was ugly sweater Christmas parties. Whoever came up with that idea needed to be shot, or at a bare minimum given twenty lashings of the birch, his preference was for the latter.

He looked down again at the undersized monstrosity he'd squeezed his six-foot hulking frame into only an hour earlier. He pulled at the elf-green collar. It was itchy and cutting off his circulation. His wife, Sara, had laughed hysterically as he came out of the bathroom to show her what it looked like. The damn thing was a bright Santa Claus red with white snowflakes. It had a green collar and a giant 3D gold satin bow mounted on the front. It was the most hideous sweater he'd ever seen. "I look like a walking Christmas present," he said, trying to hide his own amusement.

She slapped his arm playfully. "That's the idea. Oh, Tess will love this."

Tess Hudson, Sara's longest and could be debated, most annoying friend, had phoned that day to remind her about the party. For a while, he thought she'd forgotten. Nope. Tess just loved to stir the pot. If Tess jumped off a cliff, Sara wouldn't be that far behind her. She was like her shadow.

Sara had grown up in Castine, Maine. Her parents owned the Manor Inn, a gorgeous nineteenth century home that catered to summer travelers. They'd met after he'd ferried a plane to Maine from Florida, which was where he originated until their paths crossed.

The rest was history.

Seventeen years and two kids later, they were just another American family; barring what he did for a living which took him to far-flung locations as a ferry pilot.

"Come on, let's blow this off. We'll get some beers, have a games night and—"

He went to remove it and she tugged it back down.

She screwed up her face. "No, don't be a killjoy. You said you would go. It'll be fun. Everyone will be there."

"Exactly," he groaned. The humiliation. He could already hear them yukking it up at his expense. Sara got this sour look on her face, the one that made it clear he was pushing the envelope. It was a squint in the left eye. He was sure all ladies had it. It had taken a few years to pick up on it but now he'd become quite adept at seeing the warning sign. He knew he had roughly a minute or so before she lost her cool.

"Landon, it's not going to kill you to attend one event. Besides, you missed last year. And it's not like you're going to be the odd one out. We're all wearing them," Sara said, trying to convince him that made it bearable. It didn't but how could he fight her on it? He'd bailed on the previous year, and had foolishly promised to be at this one.

Oh, how those months had flown by.

The crazy shindig was held every year at the town hall

for local business owners, and put together by that douche Hank Thomas who would get liquored up and then flirt with everyone's wife. He was an embarrassment not only to himself but to Rita who, for some abnormal reason, still hadn't divorced him. However the worst part was no one seemed to do a damn thing about it — well until two years ago, when Hank found himself on the end of Landon's fist.

Yep, he pushed his Don Juan act a little too far.

Now most would have cheered him on, slapped him on the back, and told him that Hank had got what was coming to him. Nope. Not this bunch of blind small-town fools.

Anyway, that was another reason why he dodged last year, he really didn't want to deal with the whispers, and dagger eyes. He could already feel them breathing down his neck and he hadn't even arrived. Landon raked a few fingers through his dark, wavy hair and splashed some cologne on his shaven cheeks. At thirty-nine he was beginning to show his age with fine lines around his blue eyes, and this kind of event wasn't exactly helping.

Still, a promise was a promise and if there was one thing Landon was good for, it was his word. It also helped that he adored his wife, and she'd been more than accommodating the year before so he felt he owed her. After hustling Max, his seventeen-year-old, and Ellie who had just turned fourteen, into the back of the SUV, they headed out to brave the foul winter weather. Along the way, they spotted a couple of vehicles in the ditch, and Jake Parish, a local tow driver, hooking one of them up. He would certainly earn his money this year. Winter was brutal in Maine. As they turned onto Court Street, Landon circled around the block, searching for a spot to park; not so close that they would be noticed but not too far as he wasn't one for hikes. It was packed, which was saying a lot since Castine was a small town with a population just over one thousand. His wipers whipped snow back and forth as they got closer to Emerson Town Hall — a clapboard, gray and white, two-story building that dated back to the 1900s. It stood out like a sore thumb among the residential homes that lined the street.

As he swerved the SUV into a tight spot between a souped-up Mazda and a rusted-out truck, Landon once again felt the familiar sinking feeling in his gut as he looked at those streaming towards the building. Sara was right. It should be fun. Parties were meant to be fun but usually ended up being nothing more than a sack of regrets just waiting to happen. It wasn't exactly the event that he hated so much as it was the people who attended. Okay, hate was probably too strong a word. Dislike, maybe? The binge drinking session represented the pinnacle, the so-called cherry on the cake of Castine residents' social lives. If a competition to see who had the flashier sweater could be deemed the pinnacle. Sara placed a caring hand on top of his and looked over. "It will be fine. Have a drink. And heck, maybe you'll forget you're there," she said getting out with an eye roll. He glanced in his rearview mirror at Ellie who pulled a face and stuck out her tongue. She loved the event just as much as her mother did. She snapped a quick selfie for her Instagram before following her mother. Then there was Max. Anything that pulled him away from his marathon gaming sessions was worse than death itself. Dark emo-style hair stuck to his jawline, a beanie hat that conveyed some kind of coolness swallowed the remainder, and a black bomber jacket was used to cover up the oh-so-uncool sweater. He had his earbuds in listening to music and was pretending to be asleep in the grand hope they would leave him in the vehicle. No such luck. Landon knew him better than that.

He reached over and shook his leg.

He didn't move so Landon shook harder.

If he had to endure the alcohol-fueled obstacle course so would he. All for one and one for all, and whatnot.

"Come on, if I've got to go, so have you."

He opened one eye and groaned. "Come on, Landon. I need my sleep!"

"And miss all the fun? And it's Dad, not Landon," he said sarcastically, hoping to extract a smile. No. Nothing. He got out, leaving him alone for a few seconds. In all honesty, he loved being with his family, there was nothing he enjoyed more, but he really wasn't much of a social bee. That was Sara's thing. It was one of the many reasons why she took over the inn after her parents retired, and her father passed away. He looked at his sweater again beneath his dark navy peacoat as he did up the top button. He didn't think he could feel anymore emasculated than he was in that moment. He wished he could be anywhere but there. But that wasn't to be. Hell, he would have rather flown a plane through the foulest weather than endure another eye-rolling party.

Maybe that was why he said yes to the last-minute call.

The phone jangled in his pocket. Landon ferreted through his coat and saw his boss' name on the caller ID. Just let it go to voice mail, he thought, pushing it back in his pocket and crossing the street. Snow crunched beneath his boots, leaving another trail of prints behind him. The phone rang again, this time drawing the attention of Sara. She knew the look when he looked at the screen. There only one person who would be phoning him two days before Christmas.

"You're not answering that. Leave it," she said.

"But—"

"No buts. You get a few days off. Let someone else do it."

"And if they don't have anyone?"

"Then he'll have to do it."

He grimaced. "It doesn't work that way."

"It does in regular jobs."

"This isn't a regular job."

She blew out her cheeks, frustration setting in as the phone rang.

"Look, I need to take the call."

She told the kids to go inside as she made her way over for her final attempt at making him see reason. "No you don't. He only calls you because you say yes, every friggin' time. For once, say no. You have an excuse. The weather is terrible."

He'd flown in worse. Landon squeezed the phone, contemplating hitting ignore and turning off the ringer to avoid follow-up calls, and there would be many more. Dougy Richmond wasn't one to give up. "What if it's important?" he asked.

"It's always important. Whenever has it not been?"

He nodded and hit ignore but didn't turn the ringer off. She smiled and looped her arm around his as they headed for the door. Four steps, that was all he took before it jangled again. He stopped walking and Sara scowled. "No. No. No!"

"It's my job, Sara."

"And we're your family. You spend more time away from home than anyone else. I mean, I think I've been more than patient, Landon, but even I have my limits. Now I'm asking. No, actually I'm telling you. Don't take that call. I don't feel good about it."

"You never feel good about it."

Her eyes narrowed, and she pursed her lips before throwing a hand up. "Fine. Take it. I should have known. You don't even want to be here anyway."

"Come on, Sara, that's being a little unfair."

"Unfair? You want to talk about what's unfair? Please. Don't even…" She charged off in a foul mood. Landon tilted his head back, ran a hand over his head and stared up at the dark sky. Snowflakes landed on his face, some filling his mouth before he answered. His screen flashed. A thin, middle-aged man with a terrible mustache that looked like dirt appeared on the screen wearing a flashy blue shirt, and silver jacket. His blond hair was swept over with a buzz cut on the sides and back. Behind him was a large print of a plane crossing the ocean.

"No. Not doing it!" he said before Dougy could get a word in edgewise.

"And Merry Christmas to you."

"Dougy!"

"I get it but I'm in a bind, Landon. You know I wouldn't ask if this wasn't…"

"Important? You are so… predictable, Dougy." He balled his fist looking towards the hall where Hank was greeting people like a parish priest. He eyeballed him and scowled.

"And you're my employee, let's not forget that."

"What if I hang up now?"

"I'll fire you."

"You can't do that."

"Give me one reason why not?"

"Because I'm the best you've got. In fact I'm the only one that is mad enough to fly some of the shitbirds you agree to ship all over the world."

He flashed his pearly whites. "And your bank account loves me because of it."

"It's not all about money, Dougy. I've got a family. It's Christmas. But you don't get that. You're single, living the high life, it's always vacation time for you. While I'm the one doing all the grunt work."

Dougy lifted both hands. "Hey buddy, I feel your pain, I really do. But this is a big payday. The client doesn't want to wait until the new year. He doesn't care about your family or mine."

"What family?"

"I got family," Dougy said. "That's actually why I'm

calling you. Otherwise I would do it myself." His face screwed up and his lip quivered. "You see my mom, bless her heart, she's getting on in years… and I don't think she'll make it through another Christmas, so…"

"Stop. Stop. Didn't you say your mother died last year?"

"No. Did I?"

Landon raised an eyebrow.

A grin formed. "Okay. Okay. I'll pay you double."

"You already have to pay me double. I'm on vacation."

He leaned back in his chair. "Man, you run a hard bargain. Okay, I'll give you two extra weeks of paid vacation this coming year. Tickets to an all-expense retreat. You can take all the family to the Bahamas, kick back and…"

"Turn off my phone?"

Dougy leaned forward clasping his hands together. "Well, maybe not turn off the phone but…"

Getting frustrated with him, he tried to cut it short. "Where is the plane going?"

He cleared his throat, seeing his window of escape. "Alabama. I need it there by morning."

"Alabama? I thought it would be somewhere on the East Coast. That's going to take me what, five, six hours to get there. And not to mention tomorrow is Christmas Eve. Sara will kill me if I don't make it back for that. I'm already in the shit for taking this call."

"What do you want me to say, Landon? Huh? Clients move the needle. If I don't jump on this, word will spread and that's not good for you, me or business in general."

Landon sighed and cursed under his breath. "And the plane? This better not be some shaky chicken coop."

"Brand new. Cirrus Vision Jet. The damn thing even has a parachute system. Something called CAPS. Don't ask me what it means but... the point is, you don't have to worry about the weather. Besides, it's just us East Coast boys that are getting hit hard. Compared to your neck of the woods, Alabama is beautiful. Heck, you might even get a suntan."

"Don't push it, Dougy."

"So are you gonna do it?"

"Do I have a choice?"

He made a face which meant no.

Landon jabbed his finger at the screen. "You owe me big time."

"You're my man."

"What about getting home? Please tell me you've made arrangements as I don't expect getting a flight from the airport will be easy at this time of the year… or last minute."

Dougy closed his eyes tight. "Shit!" He brought a hand up and ran it down his face slowly. "I knew there was something I needed to do."

"You're kidding me, right?"

"Landon, I've been overwhelmed by work."

"And by work you mean the shit that is underneath your nose?"

Dougy paused for a second, frowned, and looked like a kid caught with his hand in the cookie jar. He sniffed hard and wiped the powder away with the back of his hand. "Hey. It's Christmas. It's just a little pick-me-up. You know. A guy's gotta stay alert."

Landon couldn't believe he was agreeing to this. The thing was he needed the work. Yes, his job paid well but with college on the horizon, and the inn's renovation costs and expenses not getting any cheaper, it had all but burned a hole through their pocket lately.

"Listen, try to get a flight back; if there isn't anything, I have a bush pilot buddy of mine that makes trips this way all the time. He owes me a favor. Okay?"

Landon didn't say anything, he simply looked on unimpressed.

"I promise. I will have you back by Christmas Eve, one way or another."

"Yeah, right," he said before getting instructions on which private airstrip to go to and collect the plane. After hanging up he stood there looking over at his SUV as snow drifted down like ash.

"You said yes, didn't you?"

Landon turned to see Sara, her arms folded tightly

around her body.

"I'll be back by tomorrow evening."

She shook her head, bit down on her lower lip and breathed in deeply.

"Mom. Dad. You coming in or what?" Ellie yelled as she hurried over without her coat on. Sara turned and told her to go back inside before she caught a cold.

"I could take her," Landon said.

"You're doing a delivery?" Ellie's ears perked up.

Sara immediately jumped on that. "Out of the question! It's far too dangerous."

"It's not one of those rust buckets, Sara, it's a brand-new plane. She's never been up. She'll love it. Besides, you always said I'm not around enough and the kids suffer. So let me take her with me."

"I don't like it, Landon. No, she's staying."

"C'mon, Mom."

"No."

"Sara."

"Don't encourage her."

"What, you want her to be fearful of flying like you?"

Her eye squinted. Oh no, not again, he thought. Ellie wouldn't let it go and Sara eventually caved in to the pressure. "And Max? Why don't you take him?"

"Because it was hard enough getting him to come out tonight," Landon said. "No, he'll only whine about it. He'll make the trip a misery. Anyway, I'll be back before you know it."

Those final words would haunt him.

Chapter 2

The hunter was no stranger to death. Over the short span of seventeen years, Beth "Bluebird" Sullivan had witnessed death on more than one occasion. Understanding how it was necessary in order to survive gave her a greater appreciation and respect for life. She tightened her grip on the recurve bow as the crescent moon shone on the remote homestead and a howling winter wind nipped at her slender fingers.

Pisgah was a terrain of high peaks, cascading waterfalls and heavily forested slopes. Stretched out across 50,000 acres of mountains from the east to the western region of North Carolina, it was a mecca for the adventurous and suburbanites who longed to dip into its vast greenery only to return to the modern world of electricity. For her, though, it was much more, a backyard, an off-the-grid playground, a place to hunt — home.

By day, it lured in hordes of gawking bikers, hikers,

campers, climbers, bird watchers, paddlers and naturalists. Most trekked the well-worn paths and campgrounds, never venturing into her neck of the woods at the higher elevation. In the summer she would often see swirling smoke from campfires in the distance. However, tonight, in the grip of winter's teeth, it was all but deserted except for her, crouched in the darkness of a tall pine, still and silent.

She was clad in hand-crafted leather and a snug camo jacket, with long blond hair and ivory skin. Undistracted by the snowstorm and her precarious position on the narrow branch, high above the ground she gazed intently. Her icy blue eyes stood out like a wild wolf's, piercing and scanning the landscape for prey. Her gaze locked on the forest floor, even as her thoughts drifted to her mother's tragic death, two years prior.

Another Christmas, Beth reflected, *it won't be the same without you.* Her beautiful young face didn't reflect the loss as others might, nor show signs of the anxiety she had experienced adjusting to the new way of living.

All that had been buried, locked away.

She was hidden by a canopy of darkness as her keen eyes swept over the untouched powdery ground far below. A SIG Sauer P320 was holstered on her hip, and her hand gripped a recurve bow. She waited patiently.

It was late in the evening, close to ten, the sun had been down for hours.

Beth brought up the short wooden deer grunt to her mouth and blew it, letting out a few grunts periodically. Her ears listened intently for movement. Nothing. She clenched her jaw in frustration, her fingers digging into the bow. This had been the exact spot she'd caught two other deer that year, but she had yet to see another. *Where are you?*

She was beginning to think that something had scared them away, a black bear, coyote or another hunter. Or perhaps the deer were further down, out of sight and she would need to shift position. Even though she'd been out there for hours, patiently waiting in a wind that was unforgiving, Beth didn't shiver because she'd layered up, familiar with the drop in temperature. It was hovering in the low 20s.

Unlike previous years, they'd seen a large dumping of snow over the past few days and there was no sign of it letting up. As comfortable as she was perched in the tree stand, it was tempting to give up and call it a night; but no, they needed the meat and she was determined to show that she could do it without help. She shrugged off her momentary weakness and narrowed her eyes. There were deer out there tonight, she knew it, and she wasn't going back empty-handed, even if it meant sticking it out in the snowstorm until sunrise.

She scanned again, blew the grunt and listened.

At first, there was nothing. Then — there! Nearby. Her eyes zeroed in on the white-tailed deer making its way through the brush, stopping to chew. Its ears perked as it scanned for threats. A surge of excitement hit her as she readied herself. A smile of satisfaction lifted her lips as she watched it trot her way. *That's it.* Having been taught by her father, she knew exactly where the arrow needed to hit, and how many pounds of draw-weight was required.

Carefully, she brought up the bow and took aim.

That's it. Come closer. Nothing less than a clean kill was acceptable; she wasn't one for letting an animal suffer. The deer closed the distance unaware of her lurking in the shadows.

Beth released the arrow and it soared towards the target, striking it hard. A perfect shot. The deer bounced into the air and took off running on what her father called the death run. If it was a heart shot, the deer wouldn't last long.

Beth stepped confidently off the branch, plummeting to the soft white ground with all the grace of an Olympic gymnast. She landed with precision and burst forward, thighs pounding the earth like pistons following the trail of blood. Often, they would wait but she didn't want the coyotes to get to it first. A few hours longer than necessary and they would have one hell of a meal. Darting between trees, she slowed within minutes of starting to run.

As expected, the deer hadn't made it far, only fifty yards or so before crashing in the brush, confirming the shot had penetrated the heart, and was clean.

Beth slung the bow over her shoulder and made preparations to lug the deer back to the cabin using the leverage technique. She fished into her backpack and retrieved a six-foot rope.

Quickly, she tied it off around the front legs and head to make it easier to lift the front end of the body. After, she made a loop at the other end and attached it to a large, thick stick and then began winding it down to create tension. She turned and gripped the stick below the back of her knees and lifted, bringing up a quarter of the body from the ground. With snow falling, dragging it back would be fairly easy even for her five foot six frame.

No sooner had she taken ten steps than she heard a branch snap. She stopped trudging forward and listened. Nothing. In the wilderness and under the extreme weather conditions, branches snapped, and small animals like racoons would be out searching for food. Beth continued on through the forest, excited to show her father.

It was rare to see so much snow, and even rarer to find herself almost knee deep in powder. Trudging through the darkness with only the moon for light, her chin hung low as she tried to keep the icy needles out of her face that were swirling up around her like a mini tornado.

Another branch cracked.

This time she lifted her eyes but it was too late.

A massive weight from above crushed her, sending her rolling down the steep slope. An unseen figure clung to her as snow billowed in the air and she came to a stop twenty yards away. Bouncing up, snow in her eyes, her hand clasped her hatchet and scythed the air in front of her but by the time she could see, they were gone. She turned 360 degrees, scanning the terrain. Footprints. A trail of footprints in the moonlight led away then abruptly stopped.

She followed.

Her head tilted back but this time she was ready.

Beth lunged out of the way just as a hulking mass of leather and fur came at her. The face was swallowed by a deep hood but she knew who it was. The masked figure blocked her attempt at striking him with the hatchet, bouncing back and grabbing her arm, then twisting, and kicking her legs out from beneath her.

She landed hard, flat on her back in the thick snow. Gasping and out of breath she looked up as the figure pushed back the hood to reveal her father Rhett Sullivan. Long curly hair pulled back into a man bun, a dark goatee with a shock of white to it, and ocean eyes that mirrored her own.

"Nice try, kid, but what did I tell you?"

"Keep my head up?"

He nodded. "Bluebird, it's one thing to be able to kill, another to avoid being killed. You don't want to go through all that trouble to land yourself meat, only to have someone steal it out from underneath your nose. Now imagine if there had been two attackers. You'd be dead."

"Well, then I'm glad it was you."

"It might not be next time," he said, a serious expression fading into a smile. He extended a hand and she clasped it, pulling her up. "What had you distracted?"

"The snow."

"Come on."

She brushed herself off and glanced at him before telling him the truth. "Mother. Christmas." She sighed and he put an arm around her as they made their way back up the slope.

"I hear you. But you've still got me."

She chuckled but didn't go into it. He avoided the discussion as much as she did. It was just too painful. It shouldn't have happened and that was truth. As they reached the deer, her father looked down at it. "That's one hell of a shot. Well done, kid. You've come a long way. Your mother would be proud. I'm proud of you," he said gripping her shoulders. She knew he meant it too.

Her father had always had her back long before they bought a cabin and ventured into the Blue Ridge

Mountains to pursue off the grid living. That was thirteen years ago, when she was only four. She'd learned so much in that time and remembered very little from when they were residents in the small mountain town of Ryerson, a community off the beaten path but not far from Blowing Rock.

"Here, let me give you a hand," he said reaching for the stick.

She cut him off. "No, it's fine. I can do it."

He smiled. "All right." They began making their way back to their home situated a few miles away, higher up. There was something very peaceful to their way of life. It was simple, practical and slowly being embraced by others who didn't want to be dependent on the grid.

Although her father worked in town at an outdoor education center that trained and empowered individuals to embrace simple living, and she attended a regular high school, the focus was always on being close to nature. Of course that came with its frustrations and hardships as she entered her teen years and spent time with friends at their homes. She didn't get the pop-culture references that her friends would laugh at, and returning from a home where at a flick of a switch there was light and heat versus shoveling wood into a furnace, or using solar power, yeah, it wasn't easy but she was grateful for the skillset she'd gained, and it far outweighed being in the know about celebrities and the latest movies.   ⚔

Dragging the deer; her legs burned as she ascended a steep slope and panted hard. A wisp of air circled in front of her face like a ghostly apparition. Her father cast a glance over his shoulder and raised an eyebrow as if to make it clear that the offer to help was still there, but she pressed on; stubborn and determined.

Silence permeated except for the crunch of their boots. The common sounds, sights and convenience of the city were far away and there were times when it could feel very isolated. Fortunately she had her father, a collection of goats, chickens and her German shepherd Grizzly to keep her company. And when cabin fever crept in over the vacation months, Ryerson was only a short forty-minute hike down through the mountain if she wanted to see friends.

As they made it out of the dense forest into a clearing, their cabin and various sheds with steel roofs came into view. Their home was located on 225 acres, eight miles from Mount Pisgah and the Blue Ridge Parkway. When she brought friends up to stay on the occasional weekend they would head out to Black Balsam, Graveyard Fields, Skinny Dip Falls or Devil's Courthouse. Though accustomed to phones, internet and modern convenience they would often say they never felt as alive as they did when visiting. Parked nearby was a four-wheel ATV, and beneath a carport a snowmobile and a used Kawasaki dirt bike that her father had bought for her when she turned fifteen.

Her father used an SUV to get to work as there weren't any major roads that led up to their home. While some locals considered her father a survivalist, he was far from it. Her family knew preppers but that wasn't them. They just enjoyed off-grid living and reconnecting with nature.

The four-bedroom cabin, with kitchen, living room and dining area, was nestled into the woodland, protected from the wind on either side but exposed to the snow and sunshine from above, allowing them to fully charge the numerous solar panels that lined the roof and fed into their battery backup system. There had only been a few occasions they'd used the gas generator that had originally been installed but was barely needed nowadays.

Nearby was a small outhouse with a composting toilet, and down the side of the home a 600-gallon water storage tank that collected rainwater gravity-fed into it through a large tube. It offered plenty for cooking, cleaning and showering. In the drier months they would often get their water from a nearby river or spring, all of it of course would be purified through boiling.

Chickens could be heard clucking as they got closer. Her father made a comment about collecting the eggs for the morning before they turned in for the night. Attached on the other side of the home was a greenhouse where they would grow all types of vegetables all year round. It was one of the many places where Beth would spend her time, pruning, and picking beans and tomatoes. In the winter months they had to use poly-film to hold in the day's heat.

Bells jangled on goats as they came out to acknowledge their return, as did Grizzly who launched himself out of the house and came bounding over to see what she'd caught.

"Back up, Grizzly. You'll get your share later," Beth said.

He wagged his tail and charged back into the cabin. They brought the deer into a shed that was used for storage and cleaning. Her father would skin a deer and hang the whole carcass so the blood could drain out, then he would remove it piece by piece; rinse and smoke some of the meat, can small amounts, and then cure the rest with salt or brine. A good portion of it though would be freeze-dried.

"Look, I know this season is hard for both of us but

we'll get through it, okay?" her father said, giving her a hand to bring the deer into the large shed. "By the way, I have to go into town tomorrow and close up the center for the season. I shouldn't be more than a couple of hours. Is there anything you want me to get you?"

"Gummy bears."

"Really? That stuff can't be good for you."

She chuckled. "Some would say the same about the way we live."

"Ah… they just frown upon what they don't understand, kid. If the world around us fell apart, which is very likely to happen in this day and age, at least we wouldn't be fretting. But those folks down there — they've become so reliant on the grid they wouldn't know what to do. Heck, if the internet is down for longer than an hour people have a cow, can you imagine something worse?" She nodded. Nearly all of her friends' parents were intrigued by the free-spirited approach to living but when it was suggested that they could easily do it, they would turn their nose up or say it was too hard and cost too much. Who had the time to throw logs on a fire, or hunt for their supper when the local grocery store and Amazon gave them everything they needed?

"What if the weather is worse tomorrow and the trail's not clear?" She asked.

"I'll hike. I have to make sure it's all secure until the new year."

"You won't stop off at—"

"No. Of course not."

He said that but she didn't believe him. After the death of her mother he'd hit the bottle hard and she'd found a few hidden in his sock drawer and smelled it on his breath lately. The truth was they both missed her but drinking his way through it didn't make it easy. He still had to wake up sober the next day and face the world.

"Can I come with you?"

"No," he said in a quick and harsh tone that made her question if he was telling the truth. She knew the education center's cabins needed to be closed up for the winter but with Christmas, and snow on the ground, the bar's neon lights would shine brighter.

Chapter 3

Russ Black brought the high-powered binoculars up to his eyes and scanned the deserted road for cops. He twitched nervously while two of his guys waited nearby on ATVs. The drop-off was meant to occur sometime that day at Ghost Town in the Sky. It was a well-known abandoned Wild West theme park in Maggie Valley on top of Buck Mountain. The place had been closed since the early 2000s due to renovations, equipment failures and bankruptcy, though many said it was cursed — Russ Black called bullshit on that. He didn't believe in luck, curses or any of that mumbo jumbo. People just loved to make excuses instead of owning their crap. Not him, he was a go-getter, a make it happen kind of guy — and making it happen was exactly why he was at that run-down shithole in the middle of the afternoon. If he'd been given an exact time when the goods would arrive, he would have shown up then but the arrangement wasn't as clear cut as that. There were shifting variables.

He figured they'd kick back, have a few beers and spend the day exploring while they waited for the package that would change the future of his enterprise and catapult him to the next level of business. Okay, the package was Cayden's and he was just his errand boy but he'd figured out a way to take a slice off the top without him knowing. That's all he needed. A little something to get his side business going. After sharing the idea with Morgan Brown and Tommy Chen, two of his closest friends, they'd agreed to go in on it with him. And for a short while he could see it working out. The problem was only minutes earlier the mobile police scanner app had alerted them to a call of three youngsters trespassing in the roped-off amusement park.

Youngsters? He was thirty-four. They must have mistaken them for some of those vloggers that had been nabbed over the past few years exploring the location.

"You see anything?" Tommy Chen asked from behind

a cloud of vape. He was Chinese American, with a thin frame with a full head of slick black hair, and temporary tattoos over his face. He said he had connections to the Triad Mafia but that was a lie. The guy was adopted by the most unthreatening white suburban churchgoers that North Carolina could spit out. Still, when it came to brutality, he wouldn't think twice about pulling that butterfly knife out of his pocket and slicing someone up.

Morgan Brown on the other hand was the real deal. He'd already done time inside for beating a shopkeeper within an inch of their life, just because they'd given him the wrong change. Now that was a guy with issues. How his stocky, black, five-foot-two hulking frame managed to fit into that tan faux shearling jacket was a mystery. When he wasn't chugging back beer, he'd lift weights and inject steroids in his ass thinking he wasn't big enough.

"Nothing," Russ replied. "Hey, Brownie, you sure that damn app isn't faulty?"

He shrugged. "I dunno. Cayden says it's good, it's good."

"Oh yeah, Cayden says something, everything's true," he muttered to himself shaking his head.

Cayden Harris was notorious in the region, a man who'd established multiple businesses and had his fingers in anything that generated money. He also happened to be Russ' uncle and the only reason he wasn't working some shit job at a 7-Eleven. Of course he would remind him of that any chance he got. He'd offered him work back when he was fourteen, and was living with his crack whore mother out of a trailer. Who wouldn't have jumped at it? At first it was just doing runs for him, packages around town, that soon turned into other jobs, each one more dangerous than the last.

Up until now he figured his future would end in jail or with a bullet in his head; that was, until he started thinking of ways to turn the tables and use his position to his advantage. Yep, if this worked out today, he expected to be working for himself before the year was out.

He brought the binoculars up again and this time he spotted between the trees a white cruiser coming up Rich

Cove Road. *Shit!* He dashed over to his ATV, panic climbing in his chest.

"Let's go. It's the cops."

Chen panicked. "What? Which way?"

He fired up his ATV, it let out a rumble and pointed to the area ahead known as Ghost Town Main Street, it was the stretch that resembled the Old Wild West. It had a saloon, a jail, a hotel, a doctor's office, a general store and multiple other businesses either side of a dirt road that cut through the middle.

Like many of the locals, he'd visited numerous times, flown a drone over the site and knew it like the back of his hand. Right now they just needed to get out of sight. Chances were the cop would circle around in his cruiser and once he was satisfied the place was empty, he'd be on his way.

As they roared down the street, Russ looked back and saw tire tracks slicing through the untouched snow. He cursed under his breath. The cop didn't need to be smart to follow tracks. *Think fast.* He was gonna ditch the

ATVs around back and climb up onto one of the roofs and stay there until he was gone. Now it looked like they had two options: wait until he came down Main Street and circle around the buildings and head out the same way they came in, or cut through the forest.

Russ opted to go around back and slip down through the forest and wait it out. There was no way the cruiser could follow and the cop sure as hell didn't get paid enough to go on some wild goose chase over a simple trespassing infraction.

Their engines growled as they veered off the narrow road and bounced over the hilly terrain leaving the theme park behind. He figured they wouldn't have to wait longer than thirty minutes and the cop would be back in Maggie Valley attending the next call.

At the bottom of the slope they veered onto Pretty Ridge, a road that cut through a residential area of homes nestled in the mountain. It was covered in tire tracks, theirs soon blended in as they wound their way down. They pulled up into someone's shrouded, empty driveway and took a breather. Russ shut off the engine and Morgan laughed. "Oh it never gets old," he said. "And there was me thinking my days of running from the cops were over. Lucky we didn't stick around. I didn't like the idea of popping a cap in his ass."

Russ frowned. "And why would you do that?"

He chuckled. "You're joking, right?"

"You're packing?"

Morgan pulled out a revolver from a holster under his jacket. "You're damn right."

"What did I tell you?"

"Cayden cleared it. You think we're rolling up to a drop-off unarmed?" Morgan laughed and looked at Tommy, who looked as if he didn't know how to react. "Come on man, are you serious?"

Russ shook his head in disbelief. Sure he would carry a piece at times but he'd given him specific instructions to leave it at home. Morgan already had a bad rap sheet, the last thing they needed was cops frisking them and finding a piece on him. That led to questions and Morgan wasn't good at answering.

Morgan pulled a face. "Relax. We're fine," he said slapping the front of Russ's chest as he strolled over to the front door and peered in the window.

Russ took out a cigarette to calm his nerves. It wasn't trouble with the cops that bothered him as much as it was Cayden finding out what he was planning. He trusted Tommy but Morgan was a wild card, and he couldn't read him on the best of days. Russ looked over at the house. The home owners must have been away on Christmas vacation as there were no vehicles or tire tracks in the driveway, and the mailbox was full — a common mistake.

Needing to kill some time he got off the ATV and they went around and checked the windows and doors. All were locked barring one window that led into a mud room. "Man, people are stupid," Tommy said, lifting and climbing in. Inside they rooted through the cupboards searching for anything of value while Morgan made himself a sandwich and knocked back another beer. It was his third and he was already looking a little tipsy.

"You know what, slow down a little. I need you clear headed."

"You worry too much, Russ. Live a little."

If he wasn't two sizes bigger than him, he would have slapped him but that was why Cayden wanted him to tag along. If anyone would pull the plug and say something to Cayden it would be Morgan. Russ had to know where his loyalties were. While Tommy was upstairs, Russ went into the kitchen and leaned against the counter smoking a cigarette.

"You good about this?"

"Of course, wouldn't be here if I wasn't," Morgan replied.

"No, I mean about..."

"Taking a cut?" Morgan snorted. "You're not the first and you won't be the last, Russ."

He bit into his sandwich and slopped it around in his mouth.

"So you won't say anything?"

"As long as I get my share. I don't care if a little goes missing."

"Right. Exactly," Russ said. He walked over to the kitchen sink and poured himself a glass of water, chugging it back as if putting out a fire. He wanted to believe Morgan; he really did but he got a sense that he wasn't exactly being truthful. The problem was he'd already gone out on a limb and told him. If he wanted to throw him under the bus he could, so he had to watch what he said and that included questioning his actions, which he'd already done.

Morgan shook his sandwich at him. "I don't get you. He's your uncle. He pays us well. You're taking a big risk going through with this. Why?"

"Maybe I don't want to live in his shadow."

"You also don't want to be looking over your shoulder. Let me tell you something, Russ. When I was in the clanger, I did a lot of things to survive. Inside, it's all about who you know and who's watching your back. Connections are everything. You live and die by them.

You screw someone over on the inside, you might as well cut your own throat as that's where it ends. The same applies out here."

"But you agreed to it."

"I agreed to see what would happen. But I'm telling you this. As much as I like you, Russ, and we go way back, man, if Cayden catches word of this and pushes me into a corner for answers, I'm gonna tell him the truth."

"You'd do that?"

"It's survival, man. Not personal."

Russ chewed over what he said. After forty minutes and a few beers they headed back up to the park taking the same route they had escaped on. It was on the west side of the park and since they were spotted coming from the east, he figured that it wouldn't happen again. When they made it to the top, Russ pulled into the street and killed the engine. He glanced at his phone to see if a text had come in from the pilot. Nothing.

"Well let's take a look around," he said as he wandered down one of the wooden sidewalks in the Western town and peered into windows. Russ rattled a few doorknobs looking to enter but they were locked. Tommy was doing the same on the other side of the street.

"So where's this plane gonna land?" Tommy asked.

"Ghost Town Road."

"That tiny stretch?"

"Don't ask me; he says he can do it."

Russ looked around. "Where's Morgan?"

"He was here a minute ago. I think he went down between the buildings back there."

Russ might not have said anything had it been Tommy but Morgan's actions today had put him on edge. There was no telling what stupid shit he would do next. Still, he gave him the benefit of the doubt and continued exploring.

"You think they're really gonna open this place again?"

"That's what they say," Russ said without looking over. No sooner had he said that than they heard a gunshot. It echoed loudly. Startled, Russ looked at Tommy and hurried to locate Morgan. As they came around the corner, Morgan was at the far end looming over the body of an officer. "Oh shit," Russ said sprinting towards him. "What have you done?" As soon as he caught sight of the officer, he knew he was dead. There was a round in his skull. "What have you done?" he said again.

Morgan backed up. "He came at me. His cruiser was around back."

That meant more cops would come when he didn't call in. Russ brought up a fist to his forehead and kneaded the front, feeling a tension headache coming on. The drop might not happen for hours and they needed to stay off the cops' radar but was that gonna happen? No.

Behind him, Tommy caught up. He looked on, equally surprised. "Was he alone?" Tommy asked.

"I hope so," Russ said.

Morgan added. "We should call Cayden. He'll know what to do."

"No. He's not to know about this," Russ said.

"But he will. Maybe not today but he will."

Morgan was right. Few things went unheard, that's what bothered him. He looked up into the snowy sky, hoping, praying that the drop happened soon.

Chapter 4

It was his worst nightmare come true. "Bumped? No. That's impossible. I purchased the ticket online yesterday," Landon said, face flushed as he leaned across the counter shaking his e-ticket in the guy's face. The scrawny fellow shrank back inside his airline uniform like a tortoise, no doubt wishing he'd stayed in college and pursued some other endeavors. The delivery of the plane to Alabama had been a success. For the first time, he'd enjoyed taking his daughter with him and showing her what he did for a living. It gave them time to talk and he learned things about her that he wouldn't have had they not been thousands of feet in the air.

Everything was going to plan. He'd even managed to find two seats together on a plane heading back to Maine; Sara was elated. He would be home for Christmas Eve, at least that's what he thought. His gut told him different. It was like his inner "oh shit" meter could tell when something bad was about to happen. After delivering the plane, he'd been checking flight status updates every thirty minutes expecting to see a cancellation, thankfully his flight was unaffected.

Even as he arrived and scanned the flight information display system, he'd breathed a sigh of relief to see that his flight was on schedule. No weather problems, no mechanical issues, everything was good until he tried to check in.

"I'm sorry, sir, but we need to reschedule you for tomorrow."

"I need to be in Maine tonight," he said slamming his fist in frustration against the counter. Ellie tugged on his jacket and he turned to see her looking embarrassed. She mouthed the word *Dad* and looked around at a few curious onlookers. Landon was no idiot. He understood that problems came up, he encountered them all the time in his line of work but they still hadn't explained why he had been bumped from his flight. He was fuming. All he could think about was hearing Sara go ballistic. Now that was a phone call he wasn't looking forward to making. He lifted a hand to let Ellie know that he'd be a few minutes.

He turned back to the customer service agent. "Look, just tell me why?"

The agent looked around nervously. "Sir, I shouldn't be saying this but it's not the first time it's happened. I feel your pain. I understand you need to get home. All I can say is they probably oversold seats."

"Oversold?"

It was more common than most realized. Airlines needed to sell seats. It was as simple as that but the process was complicated. They knew not all passengers would make a flight. Some would arrive late, others cancel and then some would miss their connection due to flight delays. To avoid having empty seats on a flight they would oversell, creating a situation like the one he was having, where more passengers had checked in than the plane had seats. But that wasn't the only reason. Of course there were the times when an airline would purposely bump someone because another passenger had purchased a last-minute ticket at twice the price, and it was more profitable to accept that and give someone else an airline credit for taking a different flight. Now in theory that should have been him as his two tickets cost him an arm and a leg, but there were always those who showed up at the eleventh hour with cash in hand.

"So that's it? I've been bumped for someone who paid more?"

"I'm not saying that is what happened, sir. It's very possible that the airline has to transport crew somewhere as a priority to work on another flight, and it was a last-minute decision, or the flight has a weight restriction due to the weather."

"The weather? It's mild outside."

"Not in Maine it isn't," the agent said sarcastically.

Landon narrowed his eyes and clenched his jaw.

"You can't do this."

"Actually we can, there is a clause in the contract of carriage which lets them do it."

"Well, obviously!" He knew that and his temper was getting the better of him.

"So can I go ahead and reschedule you?"

"No. Forget it. I'll make other arrangements." He scooped up the tickets and turned and walked past the long line of people waiting to voice their complaints. Ellie hurried to catch up.

"Dad? We're not getting on a flight?"

"We're getting on a flight just not this one and not from this airport."

"I don't understand," she said. His mind was running rampant and it didn't help that a large crowd of people were swirling around him. He felt like a fish going upstream.

Baggage everywhere. Groups of people getting in the way. Voice alerts over the speakers. A bead of sweat trickled down his face. Another person stopped in front of him to look up at the flight board. He blew out his cheeks trying not to lose it. He considered himself a fairly patient man, he had to be, flying old and new planes all over the world, but even he had his limits. And the worst part about it, he couldn't even blame Dougy. Well, he could but it wouldn't get him anywhere. When Dougy hired him, he'd signed off on a contract that meant he would make himself available to fly planes even if it cut into his vacation time. Of course Dougy said it would never happen. He lied. It was the reason why there was so much tension between him and Sara. She knew what she was getting into when she married him but like anyone who dives in at the deep end, it was hard to know how you would feel once you got wet.

"Just stay with the bags while I make a quick phone call."

He took out his phone and called Dougy. It rang multiple times but he got no answer. Oh great. New York. Christmas Eve. He was probably pie-eyed in some bar in downtown Manhattan with his phone turned off or he was purposely ignoring it to avoid an argument. Landon tried again. This time he answered.

"Landon, buddy, old pal."

He sounded two sheets to the wind. In the background were the drone of music and women's laughter. Probably a strip joint. He'd taken Landon to one without telling him and ordered him a lap dance. After that he refused to go with him anywhere.

"Yeah, yeah. Look, I need you to contact your friend. I've been bumped from my flight."

He burst out laughing which was exactly what Landon expected to hear. No sympathy, just finding it all amusing. Why? Because he wasn't in the same situation. "Bumped? Did I hear that right?"

"Dougy. Make the call!"

"All right. All right. Calm down. Go get yourself a beer and I'll phone you back once I talk to him."

"And Dougy. You better come through. Remember you owe me."

"Yeah. Yeah. Whatever."

He hung up and Landon ran a hand over his head and exhaled hard as he glanced at Ellie who was perched on the one bag Sara had forced them to take in the event a situation like this happened. *I'm not having our daughter stuck in Alabama without clothes,* she'd said. Landon walked over, adjusted his jean shirt and undid the button on the white T-shirt below it. Ellie was wearing a black flower-print dress with a wide-brimmed brown hat, bangles and long necklaces, looking very bohemian. Over the top of that she had a retro-style boho jacket with a fur-lined hood, and brown knee-high boots. Sara wore similar outfits, though usually in the summer. Landon had told her to put something warmer on but that was like trying to convince someone the sky wasn't blue.

"You thirsty?" He asked.

Ellie scowled. "You know, you could have been a little more patient with the guy."

He groaned. "I know. I just…" he trailed off thinking about making the call to Sara. He'd hold off until he knew what arrangement Dougy had made. If he could still get back in time there was no point causing her any stress, or putting a bull's-eye on his forehead. He already had enough to deal with. "Look, I could use a drink," he said motioning to a small café a few yards away. He rolled the luggage over and Ellie found a table amid the crowded place. He ordered a coffee, and she got a green smoothie with a bagel. He pulled out a pack of cigarettes and placed them on the table.

"You can't smoke in here."

"I know that. They're unopened."

He'd been trying to give up for the past two years unsuccessfully. Long flights across the ocean, frequent stress and daily anxiety about life kept him from quitting, at least that's what he told himself. He'd tried vaping, patches, hell, even hypnotism audios that Sara had given him but none of it worked. He'd quit for a day or two then find himself buying another pack. He'd go through the same routine. He'd purchase it, and not take the wrapper off, hoping he could deceive his brain into thinking he had one. It didn't work.

"Mom know?"

"No. And don't say anything either. She thinks I've been off them for the past two months."

Ellie snorted, flicking through her phone and updating her pals through social media about their predicament. "Don't be posting anything about the flight. Mom might see it."

"She doesn't view my social media."

Landon raised his eyebrows.

"Oh man. Are you kidding me?"

"You're only fourteen, Ellie. There are all kinds of creeps out there browsing social media accounts."

"Yeah, like you two," she said before laughing.

He smiled and leaned forward. Despite the setback, he'd enjoyed the quality time with her. She made him laugh and kept life light. While parents weren't supposed to have favorites and he didn't, some could have built a case against him that made it look like he favored her over Max, but that wasn't true. It was just that he and Ellie had more in common. They liked similar styles of music, she was into old-school stuff like Springsteen and Muddy Waters, they both liked the same movies, eighties flicks, and they were often found watching one a week. Max on the other hand kept to himself. Landon had tried reaching out to him but he was always playing computer games and Landon didn't have the time or patience for that. Still, he tried but Max could tell he wasn't into it and so he'd turn him down when he would ask him if he wanted to play a PS4 game.

Landon's phone jangled. It was Dougy.

"It's all arranged. I've got your back. Dustin Chapman is his name. I've sent the coordinates to your email for where to meet him. Be there around three and he'll have you back in Maine for nine o'clock, give or take. I know it's not the best time but at least you'll be home on Christmas Eve."

"Coordinates? Isn't it a private airstrip?"

Dougy burst out laughing. "A private airstrip? He's a bush pilot. His airstrip is anywhere he can safely land." He laughed again. "By the way, he's quite the character but with both of you being pilots I'm sure you'll get on like a house on fire. Oh, and thanks again, Landon. I really appreciate it. Merry Christmas."

"Yeah, well look…"

Before he could get the words out Dougy had hung up. Landon grumbled under his breath, squeezed his phone tight and then brought up his email. There it was. He opened it and squinted. What the heck was this? He'd given him longitude and latitude coordinates that went to some farmer's field in the middle of nowhere. Was this some joke? Landon glanced at his wristwatch. It was just after one in the afternoon, and according to Google it would take at least an hour to reach the location and that was if they were on time. He tapped the table. "All right, kid, drink up, we need to leave."

"Now?"

"Yeah, and I need to find a cab that can take us."

He knew those outside the airport wouldn't drive that far so once again he was faced with having to make his own way. He made a mental note to send Dougy the bill. He got up and wandered to the bathroom while he brought up a list of long-distance taxi firms. He would have rented a car if the location was anywhere near a drop-off but it was in some backwoods rural area where the closest small town was five miles away and all they had was a general store. If the guy could land practically anywhere, why there?

* * *

"Hey mister, you sure this is the place?" the taxi driver said over his shoulder on the last stretch of road. Although they'd got stuck in traffic on the way out of the city, the cabbie's crazy driving had made up the lost time and they were roughly twenty minutes out from Dustin's arrival.

Winters were extremely mild in Alabama compared to Maine. He'd even cranked down his window because the cab's air conditioning unit wasn't working. He looked above searching for a plane. Blue skies and a few fluffy white clouds were good signs. At least they had that working for them. He couldn't say it would be the same the further northeast they went but he'd flown in crap weather before.

He was just worried about Ellie. She wasn't used to

turbulence or any of the usual noises a plane might make. Even in the new one they'd delivered he'd caught her gripping the seat tightly, much like Sara the first time he took her up. She only flew with him once.

Landon leaned forward looking ahead and then at his phone. "Yep, it's just over there."

"A strange spot to catch a plane," the guy said.

"You're telling me," Landon replied looking at Ellie who looked content. That was the great thing about kids. They didn't care as long they had their phone and their music, and their bellies were full. The cab veered off the main road onto a dusty road that looked as if it had been created by a tractor.

"You might have to get out and walk from here," the taxi driver said after a couple of minutes of bumping around. He nodded and the driver eased off the gas. Landon had already paid online so he just thumbed off some cash as a tip before getting out. The driver retrieved the single piece of luggage, bid them farewell and left them standing in the middle of the field. Dust billowed up into the air as the cab returned to the main road.

"Well, they won't believe this unless I take a photo," Ellie said. "Here, come on, Dad, get in on this one." He put his arm around her and she snapped a shot of them close up with miles of grassy fields behind them. Beyond that was a forest but that was it. No town, no bus stop, nothing, just wide-open space.

"Don't post that until we're home," he said.

"I couldn't even if I wanted. No signal out here," she said holding it up to try and get a bar. They remained there for another fifteen minutes wondering if this was just some Christmas gag of Dougy's before Landon heard the familiar hum of a plane's engine. A speck of blue and white grew in the distance as their shaky transportation arrived.

Chapter 5

Dustin Chapman looked like Willie Nelson. A shocking white beard, weathered cheeks and two long dark-haired braids poked out from underneath a red skull bandanna. He hopped out of the small single-engine plane, a half-smoked cigarette in the corner of his mouth, wearing a ratty looking black T-shirt with the name of his company printed on his chest, and faded blue jeans. As he ducked under the wing and came around, Landon noted the registration number of N9820V on the side of the plane.

Landon waved at the man. "Hey there."

"You must be Landon Gray. Hope you haven't been waiting too long?" he said extending a hand and shaking his. "Dustin Chapman. At your service."

"No, not long. I appreciate you doing this."

"No problem, glad to help out. I'm going that way anyway, so…" he trailed off cutting his daughter a glance.

"And who might this lovely young lady be?"

"Ellie. Ellie Gray," she said before Landon could introduce her.

"Well Ellie. You ready to go up?"

"It'll be her second time," Landon muttered.

"Is that right?" he said, a broad smile forming. "You enjoy flying out here with your old man?"

She nodded, pursed her lips and glanced at him. With every passing year she looked more like her mother. "Well let's get you loaded up. That's the only baggage you got?"

"Would have been less if I had my way."

Dustin smiled. "Ah, your wife packed it. I know all about that. If Mrs. Chapman had her way, I wouldn't be able to carry anything in this bird. It would be loaded down with my entire wardrobe and bathroom."

He opened the door on the side of the plane and lifted the suitcase in with ease, stowing it behind one of the six seats. "So this is yours?" Landon asked knowing that many of these guys worked for a larger company and the planes were used for business only.

"One hundred percent. A Helio Courier. You got your own?"

"No, I mostly fly for Dougy. So you're used to landing in tight spots?"

Dustin chuckled as he helped Ellie into the plane. "This bird can land at 30 mph on less than 500 feet, and believe me it's seen worse landing strips than this."

"Oh yeah?"

"I fly out to some remote locations. Not all of them provide a lot of space when you land. This beauty lands on a dime."

"I noticed. So when you're not rescuing pilots like myself, you chartering?"

"Something like that," he said looking distracted. Landon went to hop in and Dustin put out a hand to stop him. "Payment first."

"But Dougy said you owed him a favor."

"I do but I still need to put gas in this thing."

"Dougy said it was covered." Landon reluctantly took out his wallet. "I've only got forty bucks."

"Well shit, it looks like you've got a long way to walk then."

"What?"

Dustin burst into laughter and slapped him on the back. "I'm just kidding. Put your wallet away. Man, the look on your face. Get in," he said, roaring with laughter. Ellie thought it was amusing as Dustin closed the door behind him and went around to his side. On any other day Landon might have seen the funny side but his nerves were on edge. Dustin got in and put on his headphones and cranked the engine. He flicked a few switches, adjusted a couple of knobs and the three-bladed propeller spun to life. The plane rolled out over the uneven surface causing them to bounce in their seats. "Make sure your seat belts are on and hold on tight," he said. "Takeoff can be a little bumpy."

As a pilot familiar with the ins and outs of flying, it was clear that Dustin had been at this a while as his demeanor was relaxed. While Dustin was preparing to take off, Ellie announced she had a phone signal. "Finally.

Just in time too. I've got to take a photo of this as we go up." Seeing the opportunity to phone Sara, he placed the call just to let her know that they would be running a little behind. He breathed in deeply and dialed only to find himself getting put through to the voice mail.

"Hey, it's me," he said. "We should be back in Maine around nine, give or take. Though it might be a little later before we arrive home so don't wait up." He paused for a second as the plane lifted and hit a rough patch of air. "Look, I'm sorry about the way we left it. Ellie is fine. She loved the flight and I got you and Max a nice gift from Alabama so…" he trailed off thinking he was trying too hard. Even though she'd let him go, he knew her better than that. He'd spend the next few days under her glaring eye and have to make up for it in other ways. "Anyway, I love you. See you tonight."

Landon turned off his phone and stared out the window as they climbed.

Ellie was texting, oblivious to the minor turbulence.

Dustin glanced over his shoulder at him and pitched

the plane a little higher. "So you been ferrying planes long?" he asked.

"Too long," he replied.

"You must have seen a lot of countries in your time?"

"A fair amount," Landon said as he sent a text to Dougy, asking for more time off. He was looking for any way to make it up to Sara. A few days off wasn't enough. He didn't want to come back until the new year. Though the chances of that happening were slim to none. In their line of work, there wasn't a slow period. Clients ordered planes before Christmas and after, and most weren't patient.

"You thought of doing something different?"

Landon spoke loudly so he could hear him. "At times, though I'm not sure what I would do." The world below looked like a colorful tapestry or a patchwork quilt. That was the upside to being a pilot, no two places looked the same.

"You should move to Alaska," Dustin said.

"Alaska? Is that where you're based?"

"I was but a few things came up and I decided to work for someone who paid more. But when I was up there, I loved it. I worked for a lodge that offered Alaskan excursions and adventures for those wanting to take photos of the wilderness and reach spots you can't by land."

"Oh yeah? Sounds like magic."

"It is. Flying into St. Elias National Park, or taking folks over the Wrangell Mountains. Some of these places you can't get to by foot even in the summer. It's quite something to see. Here, take a look," he said reaching down between the seats and handing back a small camera. Landon turned it on and flipped through gorgeous images of snow-brushed mountains, forest, blue rivers and sandbars that stretched for miles. He'd been to Alaska twice to drop off planes but had never really had the time to explore it, and he didn't figure Sara would be up for relocating. She was a homebody, a small-town girl who liked to dream of adventure but when it came down to it, she would have a panic attack if they ventured beyond

Maine. Him, he'd always wanted to experience wild, rugged terrain and live off the land but the need to make money had always kept him traveling through life at a hundred miles an hour.

"Nice," he said handing back the camera. "It didn't pay well?"

Dustin shrugged as they flew over a huge blue lake below. Landon nudged Ellie and she looked up from her phone and smiled. It felt good to have someone else to share the views. That was the only downside to traveling alone, he'd see so much beauty but showing a picture on a phone was a lot different than soaking it in from thousands of feet in the air. It just didn't compare.

"The wages were fair but I'm getting on in years and I didn't see myself settling down in Alaska. I wanted to be closer to family. My parents are gone, and I only have one brother. Carting adventurers around Alaska was great while I was young but it didn't really give me a chance to squirrel away a nest egg so that's what I'm doing now."

"No, I hear yah. So what's paying more?"

"I deliver packages. In fact that's why I said I could take you. Did Dougy tell you about that?"

"No he didn't," Landon said, his brow furrowing. That meant delays which meant they weren't likely to get home until at least midnight.

"Yeah, I have a drop-off in North Carolina, then another in Maine and one more in New York. Hope you don't mind. It shouldn't take too long. Flight time should be around seven hours with the drop-off, refuel and whatnot."

Landon nodded as he continued.

"We'll head up to around 8,000 feet and cruise east over the Nantahala National Forest before coming down in Maggie Valley. You been there? North Carolina?"

"Once. A long time ago."

"Ah, you'll love it, it's beautiful around this time of year. Anyway, once I've delivered that package, we'll head up over the Appalachian Trail. Now that is something else. A friend of mine hiked it back in '72. Took him six months, can you believe that? Six months. Apparently, people do it every year, starting between March and April. Some heading northbound from Springer Mountain in Georgia, others heading south from your neck of the woods. What's that mountain called?"

"Katahdin."

"What's that?" he yelled over the noise of the engine.

"Mount Katahdin," Landon replied. "And yeah, I know about it."

It wasn't far from Castine and he'd met a number of people who hiked the trail but never completed it. Landon sank back in his seat and reached over placing his hand on Ellie's shoulder. "You good?"

She nodded, gave a smile and then asked if she could get her tablet out of the luggage. "Yeah, should be okay. Just buckle up in the back, okay?" She unbuckled and slipped between the seats into the last row. Landon heard the zipper and then her fumbling around.

He stared out the window as Dustin continued. "Hey, look, I can hook you up with the guy I work for if you like? Who knows, maybe you'd like it. The beauty of this job is you land, drop off a package and head out again. It's easy money."

"What's in the packages?"

"No idea. I don't ask and I don't look."

Landon frowned. There was no chance in hell he would go up in the air without knowing that kind of information. It was safety 101, but then looking at Dustin, he figured he was at an age he didn't care. Desperation could make the sanest people do crazy things.

"You don't know what you're delivering today?"

"Nope," he said. "I don't want to know. It's none of my business."

"And yet you're the one on the hook if it's illegal."

He burst out laughing. "It's not illegal. I wouldn't get involved in that kind of stuff."

"Well then why aren't they shipping it via FedEx?"

Dustin glanced at him before checking his instruments. "Don't know. Don't ask."

Landon didn't like the sound of that but before he

could say any more the plane banked to the right and changed course and Dustin muttered something over his headset. It didn't take long before they were flying over Georgia and the Great Smoky Mountains National Park. Dustin had to point it out as not only had the sun disappeared but it was hard to distinguish as it butted up against the Nantahala and Pisgah National Forests. However, he seemed convinced he knew where he was. Far below they could see mountains and green for miles. The drone of the engine vibrating the plane made him close his eyes.

They continued flying until the sun dipped below the horizon.

Dustin was in the middle of telling them where they would be coming down when the engine spluttered. Landon had heard that sound before. He'd run into a number of issues delivering rust buckets and it was never good to hear. But that wasn't the worst of it. He opened his eyes to see the instrument panel had gone dark. No lights. Nothing. What the heck?

"Dustin? What's going on?" he asked in a calm and controlled manner trying to not to scare his daughter. He had a rough idea but he hoped Dustin had just flicked the wrong switch or was pulling some kind of prank. But no.

There was no power.

"I don't know. It just went blank."

He gripped the yoke tight trying to control the plane as it glided through the clouds, quickly losing altitude. Landon leaned forward, shouting out a few things for him to check, his years of experience kicking in. Nope. All signs were pointing to an electrical failure. The upside to being inside a single-engine plane was that it was possible to glide and land safely. He'd done it once in his years as a pilot, but that was years ago and it scared the crap out of him.

Still, they were losing altitude fast.

"Dad. What's going on?" Ellie said.

For a second, he'd forgotten she was there. So used to flying alone, he'd only ever had himself to worry about. Fear shot through him. "Ellie, get back in your seat," he said as she unbuckled to try and make her way from the back seats to the front. Dustin was doing everything he could to bring it down in a controlled manner. He was yelling out that they'd flown past the drop site and they were now over the Pisgah National Forest. Few pilots with their years of experience panicked but this was definitely one of those moments.

"I'm gonna try and bring it down safely but…" Dustin trailed off and Landon knew what that meant. He was flying blind. It was one thing to have the electronics go out and fly by what was known as VFR, another to be flying over a blanket of darkness with nothing to guide them. It was pitch dark outside. No city lights. No headlights. Nothing. It was as if the world had gone black. Landon leaned back in his seat and tried to calm his daughter but it wasn't working. She was terrified and rightly so. The odds of survival were extremely low and that was with all the instruments working but at night, and with no references to determine how high they were, there was only one thing left he could do — pray.

Chapter 6

Thirty minutes earlier…

The weather had taken a terrible turn for the worse. Beth gazed out the window at the whiteout conditions as she waited for her father to return from town. All she could see was snow blowing and swirling. He should have been back hours ago. He'd left early that morning just as the sun was coming up and had promised to return before dusk. Still no sign of him. Grizzly let out a whine. Beth ran a hand over the dog's head. "I know. I know, boy. We'll give it another fifteen minutes and then I'm going down."

She crossed the room, took a seat at a wooden table and turned on the radio to get the report from the National Weather Service. Static came out of the speakers and then she dialed into the frequency.

A SEVERE WINTER STORM SYSTEM WILL MOVE THROUGH PARTS OF NORTH CAROLINA, WITH THE WORST CONDITIONS OCCURRING ACROSS THE BLUE RIDGE MOUNTAINS AND PISGAH NATIONAL FOREST... THE WINTER STORM WARNING IS IN EFFECT STARTING THIS EVENING AND IS EXPECTED TO LAST UNTIL LATE TOMMOROW... ACCUMULATIONS OF 12 TO 22 INCHES AND WINDS UP TO 60 MILES PER HOUR WILL CREATE BLIZZARD CONDITIONS.

EXPECT MINIMAL VISIBILITY AND ONLY TRAVEL IN THE CASE OF AN EMERGENCY... THOSE THAT MUST TRAVEL ARE BEING ADVISED TO TAKE EXTRA BLANKETS, FLASHLIGHTS, FOOD AND WATER IN YOUR VEHICLE... AND DUE TO THE SEVERITY OF THIS WINTER WEATHER, VENTURING OUT ON FOOT SHOULD BE AVOIDED AT ALL COSTS.

Beth switched it off and brought a hand to her forehead. She hoped to God that her father wasn't passed out in some drunken stupor or worse — had taken a fall somewhere on the mountain. He was more than capable of surviving under the worst conditions but that was if his mind was clear. As of late he'd been hitting the bottle a little too frequently and that could easily cloud his judgment. She crossed to the fireplace and tossed a few more logs on the fire. The wood crackled and popped, shooting out a few golden embers that hit the fireplace screen.

Grizzly padded over and she wrapped an arm around his huge frame, nuzzling her head against his. Having lived for so long on the mountain with her father she wasn't afraid, her father had made sure she knew how to be self-sufficient from an early age, but that didn't mean she didn't worry. Her mom had been his world. There wasn't a day that went by that she hadn't seen them snuggling up to one another and him kissing the crook of her neck.

Heading down the mountain would go against her father's wishes but she'd all but run out of patience. "Screw it, I'm going," she said heading over to bundle up in a thick coat that she'd made herself from elk hide and sheep's wool. It beat any of the expensive winter coats they sold in town. Her father had taught her how to clean, gut and skin a deer, then her mother had shown her the process of tanning a deer hide. Nothing went to waste. Unlike hunters who killed for sport, in their world it was all about survival. Grizzly went over to his leash and picked it up in his mouth.

"No. I can't take you, boy. The weather is too bad and it's faster if I go alone. You stay here, it's warmer."

He dropped the leash near her feet and gave her those puppy eyes. He wasn't a pup anymore and was closing in on five years of age but he could still melt her with one glance of those big brown eyes. As the storm was getting worse and there was a chance she might get lost or caught in it, she considered collecting her backpack — the one that she took on weekend hiking excursions in preparation for her trek of the Appalachian Trail next year.

It was lightweight, no more than 20 pounds and contained the essentials she might need in the event she ever got lost or stranded: shelter, sleeping bag, sleeping pad, food, water container and some additional clothes. There were other items in there like a first-aid kit, a fixed blade, fire starter, water purifier, headlamp batteries and so on but the first items were the main essentials. The rest usually could be picked up along the way in different towns. The key was not to overload the pack, far too many hikers did that and the mountains were littered with items that hikers had tossed out of their backpacks.

She scooped it up, pulled her hood over her head, slipped into her thick waterproof boots and grabbed up her bow before heading to the door. Grizzly let out another whine and she looked back at him. "It's too cold, Grizzly. Dear me, Dog, you don't let up." He dashed to the back of the room and she smiled when he returned with a black bag that contained small boots for dogs. He was too damn smart for his own good. They were waterproof and anti-slip and he looked ridiculously funny in them but her mother had got him used to wearing them since he was a pup. They only put them on when the weather was really bad. He dropped the bag and she groaned. "Uh. Grizzly, it's not just cold it's deep snow. Far deeper than those boots. Besides you won't be able to keep up. Now go on back to your bed. I'll be back soon."

She would have taken him had it been just a light dusting of snow but one glance at the thermometer hanging outside and it was clear the temperatures had dropped considerably since the morning. The dog padded back to his bed. He turned a few times and settled in. "Good dog."

Beth scooped up ski goggles and gloves, readying herself for all that Mother Nature had to throw at her. A gust of wind nearly knocked her over as she opened the door and forged ahead. *This was the kind of weather people died in,* she thought.

Her father had taken the ATV so she hopped on the

snowmobile and fired it up.

Snow kicked up behind her as she roared off down a trail on the side of the mountain, the motor groaning beneath her. It wouldn't take long. She'd head over to the outdoor education center and if he wasn't there go on to Dazzles, the one and only bar in town.

The blizzard was worse than she thought. Every bump and curve threatened to hurl her. She sucked in air quickly trying to catch her breath. The initial onslaught of snow blasting her in the face nearly flung Beth clear off the back. They'd experienced snowstorms before but nothing like this. She tightened her grip on the handlebars, slaloming around tall pine trees. The glow of the machine's halogen headlights bounced and illuminated the way but because the barrage of snow was so hard, it was like smashing through one wall of white after another. She eased up on the throttle but only to make sure she was still on the trail. On a regular day she would joke with her father that she could have navigated to the foothills with a blindfold on but she was quickly learning that maybe it wasn't as easy as she thought.

Another sharp gust stole her breath filling her lungs with frigid air. "You better not be drunk," she said.

If she found him lying in a pool of vomit on Christmas Eve, she was going to lose her shit. She tried to convince herself that her father had simply taken cover inside the outdoor education center and was planning on returning when the wrath of the storm had calmed. She'd even thought that he could have stopped to help someone who might have broken down. That would have been just like him. A good Samaritan, always thinking of others. It was what had driven him to his current line of work — that and his love for nature.

Beth slowed almost to a crawl and turned to her left and right. Damn it. Had she left the trail? It all looked the same. After a certain point she could usually see town lights flickering in the distance but there was nothing. It was just complete white.

She tried to calm the beating of her heart and slap away the thought that she was lost. Navigation was a strength of hers. She looked up towards the stars hoping to use them as guidance but she kept blinking hard from so much snow falling.

The compass.

The snowmobile idled as she reached into the backpack and pulled it out. Holding it out in front of her, she had to keep wiping snowflakes off the surface. The town was south and their cabin was on the northwest side of the Blue Ridge Mountains. While she could tell that she had veered slightly off course, she was still heading in the right direction. Down. It was as simple as that — follow the slope and eventually she would hit Jackson Road, five minutes later she would be on Main Street.

Putting the compass back into her bag, she took off again, this time confident but yet concerned that she wasn't seeing lights. There were always lights. The engine growled as she bounced over a crest then yanked the handlebars, narrowly missing a tree that exploded into view. For a moment, Beth was positive that she'd lose control of the Ski-Doo and collide with the thick trunk.

Thankfully, the tread raked at the snow and she stayed upright and was able to veer her way to safety.

Relieved at the near miss, she soldiered on in near-zero visibility, maintaining the same southeasterly line. Her hands were so tight on the handlebars that they felt like they'd frozen.

Suddenly, it happened. The wind howled in her ears so loud that she didn't even hear the plane until it was nearly upon her. An explosion like a thousand fireworks going off. Fear shot through her as her eyes lifted at the sight of a small plane slicing through the forest like a hot knife through butter.

Her eyes widened in horror.

It was heading directly for her.

Those brief seconds of distraction were all that was needed. Another tree trunk came out of nowhere. A split-second decision; she jerked on the handlebars as the Ski-Doo caught air over a hilly section of terrain. It was too late. The collision was brutal, sending her flying off into a pile of powdery snow.

She never lost consciousness but for a moment sound became muted until she pulled her head out of the snow and gasped.

The wail of the Ski-Doo vanished beneath the roar of the plane as it cut through the forest, snapping trees like twigs, an explosion of metal and Mother Nature.

Groaning, she scrambled to her knees, her muscles burning. She'd expected a broken bone or two but had narrowly scraped through with nothing more than a sprained wrist, a few pulled muscles and some gnarly scratches. She sucked in air. Every breath felt like she was choking on slush. After catching her breath Beth scrambled back up the slope towards her machine which had flipped on its side. The engine was no longer on. Slipping and sliding in the snow she cursed under her breath at the sight of mangled metal.

"No, no, no," she cried as the headlamp on her head swept over the carnage. She wiped a wet hand across her face, lifting the goggles to get a better look. The air was solid snow. "Damn it!" She didn't need to try and start it again to see the Ski-Doo was a complete write-off.

Her thoughts turned to the plane. Had anyone survived?

In the distance between the trees she could see a speck, the faint glow of fiery orange and smoke rising up from that forest-slicing crash. Beth slipped the goggles back on and looked down; her knees were deep in powdery snow and more of it kept whipping up into her face. She looked down the mountain, still unable to see the town's lights. Something was definitely wrong. She might have veered off the beaten path but she knew how long it took until the glow of civilization came into view, but now there was nothing. *Do I head back to the cabin, continue into town on foot or go see if there are any survivors?* What would her father do?

She scrambled to her feet, pulled out a flashlight and turned it on, then adjusted her headlight to provide as much light in the darkness as possible. She plodded through the forest in the direction of the wreck, her mind racing, unsure of what to do even if there were any survivors. What if the storm had knocked out all the power in town?

C'mon, keep moving…

Beth followed the path of destruction that had cut into the mountain leaving a trail of clothes in the snow. She stopped and picked up a young girl's shirt then dropped it and stepped over large branches. A barrage of ice-cold needles blew in her face, a huge gust threatening to force her back down. The wind nipped at her cheeks so she pulled up her scarf until there was very little skin showing.

Large pieces of the plane were scattered like breadcrumbs leading her onward.

Suddenly — there it was — what remained of the plane!

She didn't just see it; she could feel the heat of the flames.

A strong wind and continual onslaught of snow tried to blind her. The smell of fuel was so strong the closer she got. What if it exploded? She circled around it shining her flashlight beam over the hollow tube of metal, trying to spot survivors, but with the night and blizzard it was near impossible. She could hear her father telling her to stay back but what if someone was alive? What if she could have saved them? The thought of that young girl's clothing made her push aside her own safety as she pitched sideways down a slope to get near.

"Hello? Anyone alive?"

No answer just thick black smoke.

Beth pressed on even as more flames licked up the front of the plane. The rear had been torn away and the nose stopped by an army of tree branches crushing the front like an accordion. Metal groaned as she shone her light inside over two seats. It fell upon the pilot and she closed her eyes. The light then washed over another figure hanging over a seat. It was a man, at least that's what she could tell. Was he alive? Beth carefully worked her way into the guts of the plane, and made her way over to the man.

"Hey mister."

No answer. "Hey!"

Still nothing.

Cautiously she reached out and just as she was about to touch his arm, his right hand clamped onto hers. "Please… help."

Chapter 7

Sara smashed the accelerator and revved the SUV's engine again, trying not to freak out. The engine whined loudly as Max put his shoulder into it. "Give it some!" he yelled.

"I am," Sara bellowed out the open window. A gust of cold wind took her breath away. The vehicle rocked slightly as the tires tried to bite the snow. For a second she thought they were free then it slipped back down the slope again, crushing that hope. Sara cursed and smashed a fist against the steering wheel causing the horn to beep. Startled, Max looked over the hood and scowled. *Sorry,* she mouthed.

They'd been at her mother's for the better part of the day, keeping her company until Landon returned. Geraldine had purchased a home on the northeast side near Wilson's Point six years ago when Sara's father was still alive. She was getting on in years but wasn't ready to give up her independence so Sara arranged to have groceries delivered and she dropped in every day to make sure she was okay. At seventy-eight, Geraldine's bones ached but beyond that she seemed the perfect picture of health. Okay, her memory was getting bad and that had been a serious concern of Sara's but the doctors were still running tests to determine if she was experiencing the onset of Alzheimer's. After her losing her dad, she'd told her mother to come and live with them at the Manor as there was plenty of space but she wouldn't have it. *Nope, you have your own family now,* she would say. *Besides, Landon wouldn't appreciate it.* Landon was never there, she'd reply.

Anyway, on the short trip home to the south side she lost control and slid into a snowbank. Max trudged up, out of breath, and placed a hand on the top of the roof. "It's freezing out here." They'd already tried salt under the tires but that didn't help. "How about I jam the car mats under the tires? It might give it enough traction."

"Forget it. Don't break your back, I'll call Parish

Towing. Get back in."

Max hopped in the back while she fished into her bag for her phone. She already knew his number. Most Maine residents if they were smart had AAA or a tow truck guy in their contacts.

Landon had always grumbled about the cold weather saying it was much nicer down in Florida but she couldn't fathom living anywhere else. She was born in Bangor and her parents had moved to Castine when she was three to run the Manor Inn. Although she'd entertained the thought of moving, she couldn't bring herself to leave behind the picturesque town that was situated on a peninsula in Penobscot Bay. And, even though it wasn't an island, per se, she and others referred to it that way. It was the home of the Maine Maritime Academy that trained up her older brother Caleb who now worked as an engineer for the United States Merchant Marine. It was also where she had her first kiss, graduated from high school and spent most of her summers with friends, the same close-knit circle that had seen her through a bad divorce until Landon came along. Since then many of her friends had moved to different parts of the country, the only one that remained was Tess.

"Hey Jake. You think you can swing by 166, I'm just past TimberWyck Farm," she said over the phone.

"You as well?" He groaned. "You're the fourth call I've had tonight."

"What can I say? They just don't make winter tires like they used to." She figured she'd blame it on the tires for once instead of the weather like most people did. The truth was she'd skimped this year and gone for all-season because they were cheaper and with the recent renovations eating a hole in their pocket and not having to travel far, she assumed they'd be fine. Famous last words.

"Look, I'm not sure when I can get there but—"

The line went dead.

"Jake?" Sara thought he'd hung up on her but then she looked at her phone, the power was off. She tried turning it on but it wouldn't work. "Ah man, hey Max, can I use your phone for a second?" She put her hand back without even giving it another thought.

"You can't. It's dead."

She turned in her seat with a frown. "What? Yours too?"

"Yeah. I was just playing a game and the damn thing shut off." He tried to power it on but it wouldn't work. As she was looking back at him, she noticed the lights in the house of TimberWyck Farm were off. They'd been on only minutes earlier.

"Huh. That's odd."

She fished into the center console and pulled out her charger unit. Although it was odd that both phones stopped working at the same time, she thought she'd try charging them. She plugged it in and turned over the ignition. Nothing. No splutter. No cough. Not even a click. "Are you serious?" she muttered. Sara tried again without success. "Oh, can this night get any worse?" A chill came over her. She knew they couldn't stay there long without heat; they'd freeze to death. Temperatures in the winter often dropped to below 20 degrees and with the freak weather they'd had over the last couple of years she wouldn't be surprised if they would see it drop even lower.

"C'mon, let's head over to the farm. Maybe someone can give us a ride back to the Manor." By vehicle it was a short ten-minute journey from where they were but by foot, they were looking at least an hour and thirty minutes and in this weather that wasn't happening.

It didn't take long to retrace their steps to the sprawling white farmhouse with a faded red barn that had sheep in the field even in the middle of winter. TimberWyck was the only working farm in Castine and while most locals were supportive, some felt it was an eyesore or a nuisance to have pigs in the road, or animals making their way into the private cemetery. Sara had no problem. She thought it was good to support local businesses and farms were just another one of them.

She and Max strolled onto the four-acre property and made their way up to the farmhouse. They heard chickens clucking, and saw a pen of ducks and turkeys, and beyond that goats.

"You sure about this?" Max asked. "Shouldn't we wait for Jake?"

"We will once we find a phone that works."

Sara made her way up to the white home and knocked on the door. Both of them shivered as a strong blast of cold air swept up snow around them. No answer. She tried again then saw through the opaque glass a light moving towards them.

"Yeah, yeah, I'm coming."

The door swung open to reveal a heavyset man in his early fifties; he was dressed like he'd just walked out of a bush. He wore a ratty brown cardigan with a shirt beneath it, and torn jeans. His hair was a mess, his chin unshaved and he smelled like pig shit. It probably didn't help that he shone the flashlight beam directly in her face. Sara squinted and thumbed over her shoulder. "I run the Manor Inn. My son and I came off the road half a mile from here, wondered if we could use your phone?"

"Why don't you walk?"

His abruptness caught her off guard. Most people she'd met in town would go out of their way to help. "Well, we just thought it would be quicker to call Parish Towing Company."

"Does it look like we've got power, lady?"

Footsteps echoed behind him.

"Arlo, let the poor woman inside." A figure emerged from the darkness, slapping the side of his arm. In the glow of the light she saw a large woman wearing a black apron. She had a full head of white hair, beady spectacles and looked as strong as an ox. "Come on in, honey, you'll catch your death of cold standing out there. Arlo. Go see if you can get that generator started."

As they came in, she recognized the woman. Sara had seen her around town but couldn't place the name. "You're…"

"Janice Sterling, darlin'. And you're Geraldine's daughter."

"That's right."

She let out a laugh as she beckoned them on in. "How is your mother doing? I used to see her in town a lot but haven't seen her around in a while since your father passed." She made a gesture of a cross on the front of her busty chest. "God rest his soul."

They were led into a beautiful but dark kitchen. Light from the moon filtered in through a large set of windows at the back of the house. The floors were stone tiles and there was a large oak table in the middle of the room with pots and pans hanging from a rack near the sink and breakfast bar. A fresh bouquet of flowers rested in the center. Janice pulled out a chair and told her to take a seat.

"Good. How long's the power been out?" Sara asked getting back to the reason she was there.

"Less than five minutes. We figure the storm has knocked out the power."

It wouldn't have been the first time. Thousands had woken to a power outage after an icy blast knocked out power and buried the state in close to two feet of snow a few years back. Her business along with 130,000 homes were left without electricity. It wasn't long before the governor of Maine issued a state of emergency. It was a pain in the ass but par for the course living on the east side of America.

"Yeah, I figured the same," Sara said not wishing to sound like she was thinking it was bigger than that. At that moment in time she had no idea. Janice lit a few candles making it easier to see her. A warm yellow glow filled the kitchen. "The thing is, I noticed our phones weren't working. Is yours okay?"

"I haven't checked yet, hon, you can try my cell phone over there if you like while I make us a nice cup of tea. Fortunately I just boiled the kettle when the power went out so it's nice and hot. You have to thank the Lord for small mercies."

She shuffled her large frame over to the kettle while Sara crossed the kitchen and scooped it up. A press of the button answered that. Nothing. "It's dead."

"Oh. Well there's a landline on the wall in the next

room."

Max looked at Sara and gave her a look like, don't leave me with this lady, but she just smiled and went to locate the phone. It was one of those hard-wired phones like the one they had at the Manor. Sara picked it up and got a dial tone. "That's odd." She wasn't familiar with how everything worked though she did know that cell phone services could become unreliable in periods of high volume like a weather emergency, and cordless phones could lose their power, but that didn't explain why their cell phones had no power. She was certain hers had a full charge only minutes before it stopped working.

Sara tried calling Parish Towing but got no answer. She assumed he only had a cell phone and was between jobs. The business was small so there was no one except Jake that usually answered. She hung up but kept her hand on the phone.

"Any luck, dear?" Janice said from the kitchen.

"Your phone works but I can't get through to anyone. Your husband, Arlo, doesn't have a vehicle that works, does he?" she asked hoping that Janice would say yes, as there was one other person she knew who might but she hesitated to phone him. Landon hated him and well… he'd swung by the Manor a number of times when Landon was away to offer his services, and she had to admit he was a bit of a handful.

"I'll go and ask," Janice said.

Just in case she picked the phone up and placed the call. Rita Thomas answered.

"Ah, hey Rita. It's Sara. Sara Gray."

"Oh Sara. I hardly recognized you."

"How are you holding up with the power outage?" Sara asked

"We have a gas generator going for now, you?"

"Not so good. We have one at the Manor but the problem is getting there. We're kind of stranded in between and the weather seems to be getting really bad out there."

Before she could ask, Rita put a hand over the phone and yelled. "Hank. Hank!"

She was kind of hoping Rita would assist her but either way would work.

"Who is it?" a muffled voice said.

"Sara Gray. She's stranded."

"Oh, Sara…" he said in a seductive way. A second later he got on. "Sara Gray. In a little trouble, I hear?"

She brought him up to speed and he immediately jumped on it. "Landon's away? Well, isn't that troubling. Don't worry. I have an old classic truck that is working. How? Don't even ask but I think it's got to do with all these new automobiles having computers. That one doesn't and I had it out on the road only twenty minutes ago, giving Jake a lift back to his business." He burst out laughing. "Can you believe that? I towed Jake Parish's vehicle back to his business. You should have seen the looks we got."

"I bet," Sara said. "So can you help?"

That was all that mattered to her.

"Give me the location. I'll be there in ten."

No sooner had she given it and hung up than Janice

said Arlo had a vehicle that was starting, but he was hesitant to take it out with the weather being as bad as it was.

"Not a problem. I made an arrangement with Hank Thomas."

"Hank Thomas?" Arlo said entering the kitchen with a scowl on his face and rubbing his hands on a greasy looking cloth. "That good for nothing better not step foot on this property."

"Oh you settle down," Janice said. She looked at Sara and rolled her eyes like she was used to his off the cuff remarks. "Look, hon, as long as you have a ride, that's good to know. While you're waiting come and have a cup of tea and tell me about what Landon's been up to lately."

She took a seat and Janice poured her a cup. As she began talking, her mind went back to that night Landon struck Hank in the face.

This is going to be one uncomfortable ride home.

Chapter 8

The single-engine plane that hurtled towards the earth was just one of several they saw disappear into the surrounding forest. Seconds later, a large 747 commercial airliner nosedived into Maggie Valley, tearing through the town and erupting in a fiery blaze. It all happened at once, instantaneously lights went out, his phone shut off and their ATVs coasted to a standstill. What came next was a series of explosions that rocked the valley. Russ' initial thought was some kind of terror attack. No power. Vehicles shut off. Planes crashing into the earth. It had all the hallmarks of an attack by some foreign group. Russia, China, North Korea and even Iran had been gunning for America for years, looking for ways to bring them to their knees. Was it possible they were behind it?

"Holy shit!" he cried out, climbing off his ATV and hurrying over to the rocky bluff that overlooked the nearby town. They'd just finished dumping the cruiser into the forest and disposing of the officer's body when he'd got word from the pilot that they should be landing shortly and to look out for a white and blue plane.

They'd seen it roar overhead before it disappeared.

"What the hell is going on?" Morgan yelled, out of breath and panicking as he made his way over through the worsening storm. The weather had deteriorated since earlier that afternoon. Their jackets were now covered in snow.

"I think I know," Tommy said, his face a picture of seriousness.

"Well?" Russ asked.

"I mean, I think I know." He looked at a loss for words as if gripped by shock.

"Tommy. Tommy!" Russ bellowed trying to snap him out of whatever daze he was in. He gripped his arm and shook him and he seemed to come back. "What is it?"

"Some kind of EMP strike."

He wiped snow from his forehead.

"A what?" Russ had never even heard the term but he

assumed it was caused by another country.

"It could be one of several things, a coordinated attack by another country, a solar flare or a nuke."

"Ah man, I knew it. I fucking knew it," Morgan said balling his fists and pacing up and down. "Our government has screwed us over. I'm telling you it's to do with that idiot they made president. His big mouth has got us in this trouble and now look at us."

Another explosion, followed by another and all three of them instinctively ducked as if they were expecting a bomb to drop on their head. Russ needed to know more. He grabbed Tommy by the jacket. "Solar? EMP? What the hell are you talking about?"

Tommy groaned and ran a hand over his face as they crouched near a grove of trees. "It could be caused by a scud missile fired from a ship. Seriously? Have you not been following the news?"

"Who the hell has the time?"

"Obviously not you. Anyway, that's just one scenario. There could be a number of things that have caused it.

One of which is that solar storm they were expecting to have." He looked back at them and they had blank faces. "Man, you two really need to pick up a paper, turn on the news, browse the internet. Holy crap."

"Yeah well, not everyone got the education you did," Morgan said pulling out a cigarette and lighting it to calm his nerves. Russ took one.

"You don't need a university degree to open your eyes and ears." He groaned. "Look, back in 1859 there was this massive solar storm that created an electromagnetic pulse. It was referred to as the Carrington Event after the guy who witnessed it, Richard Carrington. Anyway this coronal mass ejection blasted the earth and created what was known as a geomagnetic storm. The largest one they've ever had. The aurora was seen all over the world. To cut a long story short, power lines caught fire, some exploded and telegraph systems were messed up. It ended up that over five million people were thrown into darkness because of it. Now if we had an event like that today, no one would be able to deal with it. We are too reliant on our technology, smartphones, ATMs, internet, batteries, the list goes on. Most of today's world is electronic and cars are computerized… so, boom, a solar flare erupts and now everything we have relied on will vanish." He took the cigarette Morgan had given him and lit it, sucking on it and puffing quickly. His hands were shaking as he continued. "There was this news piece the other night about NASA warning that a monster solar flare could hit us in the next few years."

"Few years. Then why the hell has this just happened?"

"Solar flares happen all the time. It's just that most aren't at the level of what was seen in 1859 and some don't even hit the earth. Take July 2012 for instance — a similar storm to the Carrington happened where the sun unleashed two massive clouds of plasma that missed the earth. I remember the physicist saying that had it hit, we would have been picking up the pieces. When this kind of stuff happens, satellite communications can be crippled, and there is usually some kind of severe damage done to the power grid leading to widespread blackouts, disabling anything that's plugged into a wall socket and hell, even toilets won't flush because they rely on electric pumps."

"You sure know a lot about this," Russ said.

"What, just because I work for Cayden or chose to drop out of college, I'm supposed to know nothing?"

"I didn't say that."

"I find it fascinating."

"Fascinating enough to prepare for it?" Russ asked, hoping he would say yes.

"Well let's not go that far," Tommy replied grinning. His grin soon faded as he looked back at the town far below and the inferno that had all but destroyed the buildings. "You see that down there. If this is what I think it is, that will be happening all over the world. Planes going down I mean. They say there are over 8,000 to 20,000 planes in the air at any given time, with around 3,000 over the United States. Bring those down and forget bombing a country, commercial and private airplanes will do it for you."

At the high elevation of almost 5,000 feet, the darkness

was lit up with pockets of orange, the result of downed planes, crashed vehicles and buildings that were now on fire.

Tommy exhaled hard. "Again though, that might just be one of the reasons why this has happened. The other is a nuclear attack and without communication we'll be hard pressed to know for sure, and really, I don't think it matters right now."

"Okay but what will be working?"

"I know what won't. There will be no lights, ATMs, internet, television, refrigerators, microwaves or even hospital equipment. Sure, some places will have gas generators and that might last for a while but with no transportation running, those gas stations won't be filled up, and that goes for grocery stores."

Russ got up and paced. "No. You make it sound so bleak. Whatever this is, our military will deal with it. I give it a week and things will go back to normal."

Tommy laughed but said nothing.

"What are you laughing about?"

Tommy made his way back to one of the ATVs. "You think the military is going to deal with fried circuit boards?" he said showing Russ that the ATV wouldn't start. "You think they are going to swoop in and save the day? Even if they could do something, it will be too late. We will see a breakdown of society. It will happen fast. Maybe not today but events like this offer opportunity for men like Cayden. And you can be damn sure he will milk this bitch for all it's worth."

Russ shook his head in frustration. "Well, speaking of Cayden, he will go ape shit when he discovers the drop never happened."

Morgan walked over to him. "Never happened? How many times has he not received a drop?"

"Never."

"Exactly. He'll think it's happened regardless of this shitstorm. And you know who'll get the brunt of it?"

A sinking feeling occurred in Russ' stomach. "Us."

"Bingo!" Morgan let out a yell and kicked a piece of wood across the ground.

Russ had to think and fast. Maybe this could be exactly what he needed. A way to reset. No power. No transportation. No communication. They were miles from the small town of Ryerson. "The plane overshot us, crossed over Maggie Valley and disappeared out of view somewhere over the Pisgah National Forest. The chances of it being in one piece are slim to none. I say we go back and tell Cayden. He'll understand. I mean it's not like we're making this shit up. Hell, Dustin might not even be alive."

Both of them stared back at him stone faced.

"That's a long way to travel by foot," Tommy said looking beyond Maggie Valley.

Morgan unleashed his anger on the ATV, kicking it a few times until it tipped over. "Damn it. Damn it!"

As they made their way down from Ghost Town in the Sky, Russ was curious to know what might have survived. "Are you sure nothing will be working?" he asked. Tommy glanced at him, removing a cigarette from the corner of his mouth. A howling wind battered them on all sides. They leaned into the barrage of Mother Nature's fury.

Tommy emitted an exhausted sigh. "Some things might. Old vehicles before they were computerized should be still functioning. Anything that was kept inside a Faraday cage."

"A what?"

"It's a cage that is made of conducting material, you know like wire mesh or metal plates. Essentially it shields whatever's inside from external electrical fields. Though I imagine the only people who would have those are the die-hard preppers and survivalist freaks who are paranoid that the sky will fall on their heads."

"Well I guess they were right," Russ said.

Tommy pulled a face. "I guess they were."

"What kinds of things do people put in those?" Morgan asked, as if someone like him would have thought about it. Hell, when he wasn't doing jobs for Cayden, he was probably browsing internet porn, drinking, having sex or getting high.

"Like you care," Russ said, snorting.

Morgan narrowed his gaze as they walked down Rich Cove road which wound through the forest.

"Two-way battery-powered radios, CB radios, portable radios, LED flashlights, cell phones and so on. Basically any electronics they want to use after."

As they strode, Russ began to slow, squinting into the darkness. "Looks like we've got company." It was hard to see at first but then lights flicked on and bounced on the road. "Are those cops?"

There were two of them. Russ looked at Morgan. "That cop you killed. Did he call for backup before he went down?"

Morgan looked back at him but before he could say anything, Russ darted off the road down the slope into the forest. "You fucking idiot! This is why I told you not to bring a gun. Now look at the shit you've got us in."

"He would have arrested us," Morgan said trying to justify his actions. "I can't go back to the pen. I can't," he said.

"Well you just might."

"You know, with the lights out," Tommy said, "all manner of shit is gonna start happening. Now it's a long walk back to Ryerson. Those cops will be armed. I say we…"

"No. Absolutely no."

"Russ. There are three of us and only two of them. Morgan's armed. We distract them and Morgan comes up from behind and…"

"Kills another two cops? Are you both crazy?"

"You want those pieces?"

"I want to stay in one piece," Russ shot back.

They were taking cover in the thick brush and boulders that surrounded the road that wound down into Maggie Valley.

"It's a dog-eat-dog world," Morgan said. "I think Tommy's got a point."

"Of course you would think that. You just want any reason to kill cops."

"Well you weren't the one who was beaten up by two

of them, or had evidence planted in your pockets."

"You killed the convenience store guy, Morgan. That shit was all you. Stop making excuses."

"Ah screw you. I'm doing this."

Morgan rose.

"No, no you are not."

Russ got up to stop him but Morgan was too quick. He fired a hard right hook to his face knocking him to the ground, then jabbed his finger in his face. "You want to bitch out. Fine. But stay the fuck out of my way." With that he gave a nod to Tommy and gestured to where he was going to circle around. Tommy looked down at Russ and extended a hand but he just slapped it away and got up wiping blood from his split lip. He was tired of these losers. Tired of being Cayden's lap dog. Tired of finding himself at the bottom of the barrel scraping to survive. Tommy hesitated for a second or two before climbing the slope back to the road. He cast a glance back to see if Russ was coming but he just gave a cold stare back.

It was one thing to sell drugs, and be involved in illegal activity, another to kill innocent people. This wasn't him. He considered for a second alerting the cops, giving them a fighting chance, but that would only backfire on him. He sighed hard and climbed up the snowy bank to the road. A hard, cold wind whipped at his clothes. It was freezing outside.

"Hey," Tommy said, lifting a hand to the cops. They shone their flashlights at him and one of them pulled a gun, bringing it to eye level. "I'm unarmed. My friend and I here have a home nearby. You know what's going on?" There was at least a good fifty yards between the cops and them. The cops scanned the tree line, as if expecting some kind of ambush. They weren't wrong. Had the cop Morgan shot managed to call in for backup before he died? Russ glanced off to his right, squinting and trying to see if he could spot Morgan. Would he shoot from the tree line or step out onto the road?

"You got ID on you?" one of the cops said.

"Nope."

"You with anyone else?"

"No, I just told you, we came from a home just back there."

"What's the address?" one of the cops asked as they closed the distance. His partner had his hand on his gun but hadn't taken it out.

"The address?"

"You see, we got a call from an officer for backup before the lights went down. He said there were three men up at Ghost Town in the Sky theme park."

Tommy shrugged. "I don't know anything about that. Like I said, we just…"

Right then a figure emerged from the darkness, a flash of a muzzle, the crack of another round and both officers dropped. Morgan hurried over and finished off the one that was still alive. If asked at a later date when he thought the future had changed forever, it was in that moment that Russ knew his world would never be the same again.

Chapter 9

You'll never make it back...

Wind howled, bringing a solid wall of snow in her face as she looked up the mountain. Beth had used a snapped piece of metal to pry loose the man's legs which were trapped beneath the seat in front of him. After pulling him clear of the wreckage and bringing him to rest under a pine tree, she trudged away from his unconscious body, and returned to search for more survivors. There were none, at least none she could see. The weather had got far worse, and the sound of explosions echoing in the distance only added to the feelings of unease.

The only way to survive was to camp on the mountain. If the survivor was still alive in the morning, she'd drag him back to the cabin. Right now she needed to stay warm, get out from the weather and batten down. Her hands were freezing and snow had got into her boots, soaking her feet and making them feel like they'd been dipped in ice cream. No matter how fast she brushed snow from her goggles they would be covered with another layer within seconds.

It had been at least an hour since the plane went down. She'd managed to set up her tent in a small clearing a good distance from the wreck just in case it exploded. She didn't think it would as the weather had almost put out the fire but still, she preferred to be safe than sorry. Icy build-up frosted her eyebrows and water dripped down her back from sweat after assembling the tent in record time and dragging the stranger inside. She zipped it closed and removed her hood, gloves and boots then went through her bag to find her extra socks. Under the glow of her headlamp, Beth gazed at the man who'd been out cold ever since he'd asked for help. Outside, gale force winds punished the tent causing it to flap. She rubbed her hands together trying to stop the paralyzing cold from freezing her blood. Beth had used the extra thermal blanket in her bag to wrap the man. He looked like a giant burrito bundled up in the silver blanket and brown sleeping bag. She'd also tucked the bag under his legs to elevate them slightly.

The pain in her wrist had worsened.

She was shivering so hard that her teeth were chattering. Beth knew that under extreme conditions the best way to stay warm was to place a bladder or bottle of warm water on the major arteries in the neck, armpits and groin or huddle together but curling up beside a stranger or God forbid sliding into the same sleeping bag was something she was hesitant to do.

She also didn't know what kind of injuries he had. In the rush to drag his heavy body away from the plane she hadn't checked. Of course she guessed his one leg was broken but there was also damage to his face; blood, a good amount covered it. Would he survive the night? Every few minutes she'd lean down and listen to him breathe. Beth placed a hand on his neck and felt around for the carotid artery.

Good. His pulse was strong.

He lay there, silent and unmoving. Who was he?

Where was he heading on Christmas Eve? She contemplated searching his pockets but her fingers were numb. Oh God, she said looking up. Thoughts of her father came to mind and she wished he was here. He would know what to do. Beth unzipped the sleeping bag and carefully climbed into it. It would be tight but she needed to stay warm and her body heat would help him too. Slipping her arms around his chest she thought of the times she held her own father and gave him a hug. But this was odd. The man groaned as she butted up against his leg.

The unnatural angle of the leg made it clear how bad his situation was. She didn't want to cause him any more pain than he was already in, so she considered getting out but if she did that by morning she might be the one dead. Her stomach grumbled. She was hungry but far more tired. With the heat of his body feeding strength into hers, an overpowering drowsiness came over her. She tried to stay awake but it was near impossible,

No… don't go to sleep… stay awake… father needs you.

Her thoughts drifted as she bordered the edge between dream state and being alert. But it didn't last long and soon slumber claimed her.

* * *

When daylight broke, Beth's eyes flickered open before the stranger's. The wind was still whipping the tent but not as strong as it had been the night before. *What time is it?* She glanced at her wristwatch but it had stopped around the time the plane had crashed. She tapped it a few times. Had water got into it? A sense of relief that she was still alive flooded her. Better yet, the pain in her wrist had subsided, a pity the ache in her joints hadn't. She carefully crawled out of the sleeping bag. The man groaned. Once out she checked her gloves. They were still heavy and wet. Beth cursed under her breath as she unzipped the tent to peer out. Snow. It was the last thing she wanted to see but the weather forecast said it would continue until evening. At least the worst of the storm was over. A large amount had dumped, burying a good portion of the tent beneath a snowdrift. She looked back at the stranger.

His face was swollen and caked with blood from a gash on the bridge of the nose and forehead. Unzipping the sleeping bag to the bottom she pulled it back to get a better look at his legs. Without undressing him or knowing what pain he was feeling, it would be hard to tell what kind of internal injuries he had. But one thing was clear, his right leg was broken but at least the bone wasn't sticking out. His left leg was badly swollen, and a guess based on the bruising was it was also fractured. She hoped that wasn't the case but it was hard to know. A full examination would have to wait until she got back to the cabin. *Whoever you are, you are one lucky individual.*

Beth slipped her feet back in her damp boots and made her way out of the tent grabbing her bow. Her feet sank into the knee-high snow filling them up again. Great. Her warm, dry socks were wet now. Curious to see the plane again she plowed through the snow and high drifts making her way back. In daylight it was much easier to see. Most of the plane's remains were buried deep below snow. There was, as she had thought, no sign of life. Even if someone else had survived the crash, there was no way in hell they would have got through that night. It had been brutal. Several times she'd woken up to the sound of howling winds, and coyotes.

Realizing there wasn't anyone else she could help, she made her way back. As she got closer to the tent, she noticed a dark mass nearby.

Beth froze.

She knew immediately what it was.

It had to be at least four or five hundred pounds.

Its fur was black, and it was sniffing the ground, no doubt picking up the scent of blood. They had shit eyesight but had razor-sharp smell and hearing. Damn it. The food in her bag. She would usually tie it off with rope and put it up in a tree but in the rush to seek shelter she'd forgotten. Her hand instinctively went for her backpack strap but it wasn't there. She'd climbed out without it. It was under his legs, and the tent was unzipped.

Having lived her life in the mountains she knew the rules: don't approach a bear if you see one, don't run, keep an eye on its behavior and slowly back away increasing the distance between you and the bear. More often than not if they saw one it would just run off but this was no ordinary situation. The smell of blood was in the air. Her mind went back to what she knew. If the bear approaches, change direction. If that doesn't work, you have no other choice than to stand your ground and shout at it if it gets close. She recalled the way her mother would show her how to act aggressively and intimidate the bear, making herself seem as large as possible. *Throw rocks at it if you have to, Bluebird, but whatever you do, do not turn and run away.*

Beth could see that it hadn't spotted her. Had it just been her, she would have backed off and let it rummage through the tent but with him inside…

Very slowly she removed the bow from her shoulder and took an arrow out of the quiver. This could end one way or the other. She studied its broad back and powerful neck waiting to see which way it would go.

Don't you dare go near that tent.

The large creature grunted, and lifted its shaggy head.

Beth watched as it ambled forward following an unseen trail that led up to the tent. Behind it were numerous trees she could use as a target. The goal wasn't to harm the bear but to distract it, shift its attention and scare it away.

She pulled back, narrowed her eyes and released the arrow. It shot through the air striking into a tree a short distance from the bear. The bear let out a roar, bounced up and twisted around heading down the mountain.

She breathed a sigh of relief as her fears ebbed slightly.

Beth watched it scamper away leaving large prints behind before she pressed on and made it back to the tent. They needed to get out of there soon as bears weren't the only threat. Cougars, coyotes and feral dogs, they would all see them as prey.

As soon as she reached the tent and entered, she came face to face with him. His eyes were wide and he was sitting upright with a fixed knife in his hand. It had been inside her backpack. Obviously, he'd heard the bear.

"Who are you?" he asked stabbing the air in front of him with the blade.

Beth put a hand up. "Whoa. Put my knife down."

"This is yours?"

"And the sleeping bag and tent you're in."

"Where am I?"

"The Blue Ridge Mountains of North Carolina."

"What happened?"

She frowned. "You don't remember?"

He shook his head and she wondered if it was for the best, especially after coming across the clothes of a young girl. He groaned in agony and she pointed to his legs. "One of them is broken."

"What?"

Slowly she crept into the tent and told him she was going to unzip the bag so he could get a better look. Once she flipped back the cover, he swallowed hard and his eyes rolled and she knew he was going to pass out. Sure enough he tipped over. Beth darted in and relieved him of the knife.

She knew she needed to set the leg, especially if she was going to drag him back up the mountain which was closer than trying to reach the town.

Seeing a leather belt around his jeans she unbuckled it and began to wind it around his ankle and then her wrist. It was going to hurt like hell but it was better to do it now while he was out cold than later. Her mother's background as a nurse had given her some basic knowledge but that was a long time ago and from what she could recall that involved using a cast. Beth sat back on her heels, kneeling and observing the leg. How to do this? Maybe it wasn't hesitation of getting it wrong but fear of hurting him that made her second-guess her decision. *Nope. You need to do this.* She placed her right foot between the legs and straightened her leg, pressing her foot into the side of his groin. Beth then grabbed the right foot and breathed in deeply before looking at him. He was still out. *Here goes nothing.*

Beth yanked hard on his foot while at the same time pushing with her leg and arching back. In that instant his eyes opened, his mouth went agape and he let out a horrifying scream that echoed before he went unconscious from the pain. Another adjustment of the leg and it was finally straight again.

She needed a splint for the leg now that it was set.

It required three parts: something rigid, soft padding and some form of wrapping or covering. Her father would tell her that in the wilderness you had to make do with what you had. She could have found some branches but figured the plane might hold something a bit sturdier. Beth exited the tent and returned to the wreck to see what she could salvage. Pulling out the knife she'd taken, she cut away some of the cushioned seat which would work for padding, then collected a blanket that was tucked away below the seats in the cockpit. Finally she spent the next five or ten minutes looking for any steel rods, or metal that was firm but small enough that it could be used on either side. For a moment she thought she'd have to use two branches but finally she uncovered something she could use.

Upon returning it didn't take her long to protect the leg from further damage and ensure that it stayed rigid. A few basic knots and she smiled. *That will do the trick.*

After, she dragged him outside in the sleeping bag. He was still out cold. The sooner they could get back to the cabin the sooner she could help him. *I can do this.* She blew out her cheeks and went through the process of disassembling the tent and stuffing everything back into her backpack. All the while she scanned the terrain for that bear. By the time she was done her clothes were as every bit as wet as they had been the previous night.

Once done, she wound some rope around the top half of the sleeping bag and slung it over her shoulder. She set her face like a flint towards the slope and began to drag him back to the cabin.

Chapter 10

Christmas morning

When the second vehicle at the Manor wouldn't start the next morning, Sara knew something was seriously wrong. The town of Castine had experienced multiple power outages before, it was par for the course living on the East Coast, but this was different.

Something felt off.

The ride with Hank back from the farm the previous night had yielded no answers either. Thankfully the trip hadn't turned out to be as bad as she imagined, probably because Max was with her. Hank said he had no clue what was happening as it was too soon to know and like most, he'd notched it up to the weather. After she told him about Landon's trip, he said he'd seen a small plane nosedive into the bay when the power went out. Quickly realizing what he'd said, he backtracked and tried to reassure her that it probably wasn't him but that did little to calm her.

Still, in light of that admission she convinced herself that it wasn't Landon. He was an experienced pilot after all, with hours upon hours of flying time under his belt. No. It wasn't him. She couldn't go there, she wouldn't. That's why upon returning to the Manor she didn't wait up or fret. Nope, she curled into her thick duvet expecting him to arrive sometime after midnight with some excuse about bad weather.

However, that all changed when she rolled over the next morning just after seven and the other side of the bed was cold and empty. Her stomach sank. Sara had got up and called out to him, checked all the rooms of the house without waking Max and then attempted to text Landon on her backup phone but of course that one wasn't working either. That was when she reached for the landline. Nothing. It didn't even go to his voice mail. Getting nervous she placed a call to Hancock County Bar Harbor Airport, an hour away, figuring he'd got in late and stayed that night at a hotel.

Trouble was no one answered the phone.

Christmas or not, it was always open. *Strange.*

"Max. Get up," she yelled up the stairs before hurrying out to the woodshed to locate the portable generator. They hadn't powered it up last night as by the time they got in, it was late and both of them were exhausted. Hank had initially offered to have them stay with him and Rita but she declined saying that Landon would be home soon.

Disturbed by the unusual event, she dragged out the red generator and unscrewed the top to fill it with gas. It delivered around 7,000 to 10,000 watts — enough to power a few lights, a fridge, freezer and a couple of appliances for a few days. They'd purchased it after the big outage in 2017 that lasted a week — she'd sworn she'd never be put in that position again. Right now it was a godsend.

Bundled in a thick winter coat, waterproof boots, gloves, beanie hat and scarf wrapped around her face, Sara felt like an Egyptian mummy as she ventured out for the second time and braved the frigid weather.

The Manor Inn was set back from Battle Avenue on the west side. Situated on a hilltop with breathtaking views of Penobscot Bay, the nineteenth century inn was one of three lodgings in Castine, with hers the farthest from the downtown. With so few options for visitors, it had for a while caused some rivalry prior to her taking over the business. Since then she'd formed a good relationship by referring potential guests to the other businesses when they were booked solid. They did the same. It had worked and for the longest time they were the go-to spot for visitors until Airbnb began taking away profits with low-cost alternatives. Now anyone with a home could compete.

It had become a point of contention between her and Landon as he noted her frustration, and used it to fuel his grand idea of moving to sunny Florida. But that was not in the cards. She would rather go down with the ship than close up shop. No, instead she tackled the challenge like any business owner — head on. With high overhead and the need to stay competitive, they had taken out a line of credit to renovate, add on an addition, as well as provide free wi-fi, a restaurant and bar, a cooked breakfast, and yoga. They even went as far as to make it pet friendly to ensure that everyone was catered to.

In addition they had spent another ten grand on marketing and updating their website to highlight some of the finer points of what made them unique such as their period-style interior furnishings. Although they were only a four-minute drive from Main Street, and some wouldn't choose them, preferring to be in the heart of the town, they'd used that to their advantage by appealing to tourists and workshop groups searching for something more peaceful — a retreat that butted up against the Witherle Woods, took only four minutes' walk to reach Dyce Head Lighthouse and under ten to be at Maine Maritime Academy.

It had worked, and so far, they remained booked up several months in advance except for December to the end of February when they closed because of the winter.

Trudging back to the house Sara grumbled at the thought of having to revert to a generator. She was grateful to have it but she relied on the grid and the internet; they were critical for running the business, never mind day-to-day needs. Christmas without power wasn't what she had in mind. Landon had discussed converting the Manor over to solar power, and as wonderful as it sounded, it required more money and they were still digging themselves out of debt. No, the power would come back on soon, she convinced herself, praying that it wouldn't take a week. Still, as prepared as they were it bothered her that her cell and vehicles weren't working. As for her vehicle still in the ditch, Hank had informed her that he would speak to Jake and see what they could do but she was a realist, and didn't expect anything, anytime soon.

The generator kicked in. *What a beautiful sound.*

"Max, are you up?" she yelled again pulling her gloves off and stomping snow off her boots, then flicking the light switch. Lights came on in the house, the furnace kicked on and she breathed a sigh of relief. Christmas without power, not in this family, she told herself.

It was only then Max replied over the steps. "The internet's not working."

"That's because the power is out."

She didn't need to explain. Max groaned and disappeared in the bathroom. "No hot water either!" he yelled.

"That's because it will take a while for the boiler to reheat." She shook her head. She was doing everything she could to keep her mind occupied so she didn't burst into tears. Christmas was meant to be about family. She had plans to have all of them there with her mother, a nice cooked meal and… She sighed.

"Uh, another problem," he yelled down.

"Oh, Max, what?"

"The pressure of the water is almost nonexistent."

She groaned bringing a hand up to her head. It was one thing to deal with an interruption in TV and wi-fi, and rely on a generator to power a few appliances in the home, but to have the plumbing system go kaput, that was a whole other challenge. She recalled the town hall meeting after what happened when Maine was without power for a week. Many had shown up to complain about receiving no water while others said they still had water but it was pumping through at a lower pressure. There was a lot of confusion and people were irate until they explained.

Contrary to what most understood, even when a power outage happened, water treatment plants could continue to deliver water to homes and businesses for a short time. That was because most of them had back-up generators to keep the core components functioning, even if it was pumping at a lower pressure, however, delivery problems could arise depending on a few factors, the first being the source of water. Some received it from the city, others from a well. The second was where a person was when the outage occurred — house, apartment or farm in the countryside. They went on to explain that those living in high-rise apartments would be the first to see their water stop, while the rest were likely to see it work for a short time but at a much lower pressure.

That answer didn't suffice.

Many felt it was their right to receive water regardless of power outages and so they demanded a better answer. Town officials tried their best to calm them and explain that city water came from reservoirs, rivers and wells, and was pumped into a water tower located at the highest point in a town. From there cold water flowed naturally into homes through gravity. When the power went the only water available was what was left in the water tower. For those in homes that meant continuing to receive water for a short while but at a lower pressure, and that period of time would be shortened based on how many turned on faucets. Those in apartments would often cease to get water because the buildings relied upon a water pumping system in the basement and without electricity, the pump would stop working and so would the flow.

Unless of course they had a generator but many didn't.

That brought them to those who drew water from wells. They were in some ways the fortunate ones, at least in the sense that they were often not sharing that well with neighbors and as long as they had a generator, they could continue to pump the water into the home. Unfortunately, the Manor used city water so Sara knew it was only a matter of time before that ceased.

"Max, do me a favor, go around to the bathrooms and fill up the tubs and sinks with cold water." They had fourteen guest rooms and each one had a private bathroom.

"But it's hardly coming out?"

"I know but if we don't do it now, we might not have anything later."

She heard him turn on the tap, and the pipes let out a groaning noise. She looked up at the lightbulb above her head providing ample light. "Oh, and Max. Open the curtains. Try not to use any lights that we don't need. I don't want to use the generator too much this morning." She planned on making hot tea, and having cereal for breakfast, then heating up the boiler to take showers but that was it. It would be a weak shower at best but at least they'd have some heat. After that she would turn off the generator and conserve the gas until the evening when she could use it to power the furnace and a few lights until they went to bed. After that, it would have to be wood logs on the fire to warm the huge Manor.

As she went about making coffee, her thoughts drifted to Landon and Ellie. Anxiety had been a large part of her life even though she was taking different natural supplements to keep her on an even keel; magnesium for menopause, and B12, D, E and iron for the rest. And on the very worst days she would take CBD to take the edge off.

With a coffee in hand she took out a pad of paper and made a quick list of additional items that they needed to stock up on such as flashlights, a hand-cranked radio, extra batteries, candles, lamps, matches, non-perishable food and bottled water. Much of it she already had on hand for the running of the inn but without any idea of how long this would last she figured it wouldn't hurt to go and purchase some more. That's when it dawned on her. Oh man, the ATMs would be out. No credit card. No debit. Only cash. Fortunately she had stashed away a little nest egg after learning her lesson from the previous temporary outage. She wandered into the pantry and ferreted around for the old tea tin stuffed to the back of the shelf.

Sara pulled it out, popped the lid and fished out five hundred dollars.

No sooner was she holding it than she was startled.

"Sara."

She cast a glance over her shoulder and placed a hand on her heart. "You scared the crap out of me." Standing only a few feet away was Jake Parish. He was close to six foot in stature, broad-shouldered, dark wavy hair and ruggedly handsome. His nails always had oil beneath them from his line of work. A mechanic by trade, he ran a garage in town but had two guys working there while he towed vehicles. They'd known each other since they were knee high, both had attended the same school and rumor had it he'd shown an interest in her but for whatever reason never made a move. He had never married. She might have dated him had he asked as he was a good-looking man but by then she'd met Landon. She quickly stuffed the wad of money back into the tin but not before he saw it. She swallowed hard, raking a few fingers nervously through her hair. It must have looked a complete mess since tearing the beanie off. And smell? She didn't even want to think about what she smelled like. "Jake? How did you…?"

He thumbed over his shoulder. "The door was ajar. I knocked, no one answered."

"Oh, sorry, my mind is elsewhere," she said bringing the tin out with her and setting it on the counter. Her eyebrows shot up. "Merry Christmas!" A smile formed then faded. "If you can call this Christmas," she added, chuckling ever so slightly as she made her way over to the kettle.

"The same to you."

"So what brings you this way?"

"I brought your vehicle back."

"You did? But how?"

"Oh, Hank's not the only one in town with a vehicle that works. I have an old 1979 Scout. Anyway, I figured it was best to retrieve it now before the ice rain hits and your vehicle becomes encased in ice." He looked around. "Landon not home?"

"No, he hasn't returned. I…" she trailed off as she poured out two cups and handed him one, then her brow furrowed. "We're supposed to get ice rain?"

"If the radio is anything to go by." He nursed his cup and looked down at the floor as if he wanted to say something. Sara's stomach sank, thinking he was about to tell her some bad news about Landon and Ellie.

"What is it, Jake?"

His mouth opened and closed and he got this serious look on his face.

"It appears the entire country is without power."

Chapter 11

Darkness. Light stabbed his eyes followed by excruciating agony and a foggy haze before grimy fingers pushed pills into his mouth. His head tilted and his throat flooded with liquid. A bitter taste. Rinse and repeat. How many times? Twice, three times? Maybe it was only once and his mind was reliving it like some hellish nightmare on loop. One thing was sure, his pain subsided whenever it occurred. Waves of warmth, the sound of popping and crackling. The smell of burnt wood. Something or someone clattering beyond this gray cloud. All this was experienced at spaced-out intervals.

A fleeting memory of snow, the rustle of something large grunting nearby and then a young girl's face exploding into view. Was it just a bad dream, a state from which he couldn't wake? No it couldn't be as he kept seeing her, blurry but it was there at the edges of his peripheral vision. Sometimes hearing her voice. What was she saying? Where was he?

A howling wind. A dog barking.

Tears. Someone crying.

Water being poured. Sizzling.

The mouthwatering aroma of meat.

His fragmented mind somehow slowly pieced together reality.

A cabin, a log fire, a young girl not much older than his own. His own?

"Ellie!" Landon shot upright, arm outstretched, screaming her name, sweat pouring off him, unaware of his condition only to be reminded when pain steamrolled his body. The girl appeared at his side pressing him back into cushioned warmth.

"Careful, you need to rest."

She was strong, pretty and determined. For the first time he could see her clearly. She was no longer hidden behind a heavy coat. Her body was slender, clothed in a form-fitting green hoodie, faded tight jeans and ankle boots. Her dirty blond hair tickled his face as she leaned over to cover his body in layers of colorful cottage-style blankets. Although he was gripped by the terror of the unknown, she gave him a sense of protection, care and genuine concern.

"How long have I been out?"

"On and off, roughly twenty-four hours."

"Who are you?" he asked in his groggy state.

"Beth Sullivan. But most call me Bluebird."

Bluebird. What kind of name was that?

"Where am I?"

She looked at him and frowned. "I told you. North Carolina. The Blue Ridge Mountains. This is my home."

Slowly he said, "You look a little young… to live alone."

"I live with my father but he went into town two days ago and hasn't returned. The weather has been really bad. Do you remember anything?"

He gazed up at the A-frame wood panel ceiling. "I…"

"You were in a plane crash," she said trying to help.

His eyes roamed the room, his mind trying to connect

the dots. Then the memory flooded in, a series of fleeting images, the plane, darkness, gripping fear, his daughter Ellie screaming. "My daughter. Where is she?"

Beth looked back at him. "I only found you, and the pilot. He was dead."

"No. No, my daughter was with me," he said, trying once again to get up. "She's still out there." He wrestled for control, thrashing his arms within her grip. If it wasn't for the stabbing pain shooting up his legs, intense burning in his ribs or lack of strength, he might have managed to get up. Tears rolled down his face as agonizing grief gripped him. Even though common sense told him that she hadn't survived, without a body, his mind tormented him making him think she was out there, cold, alone and on the brink of death.

"Landon, you've broken your right leg. Maybe even fractured the other. You have excessive bruising to your ribs and your shoulder was dislocated. I managed to correct the shoulder and straighten the leg but… you still need a doctor to look at you. I've been giving you painkillers every four to six hours but I need to go into town and get help." She paused giving him a stern look. "Stay put. Don't get up. I've elevated your leg and done what I can but I need to leave now before it's too late."

"Too late?"

"Internal bleeding. You could get an infection."

He frowned. "How do you know my name?"

"Your wallet was in your pocket." She crossed the room and retrieved the battered leather wallet Sara had bought for him four years ago. It was jam-packed full of debit and credit cards, ID, and a photo of his family. Those who saw him carrying it always thought he had a lot of money on him because it was so fat but he just kept forgetting to remove the old receipts tucked inside. She handed it to him and he took out the photo and held it between his thumb and index finger. Tears welled up in his eyes at the sight of Ellie.

"You need to go see. Please. Go look. I need to know for sure."

Beth nodded. "I will. You have my word but I'm not

sure I will see much. There's a lot of snow on the ground and I only saw the front end of the plane."

He tucked the photo back in and placed his hand on hers. "Don't leave me."

"I'll be back. I promise. My dog will stay with you. *Grizzly.* He'll protect you."

"Protect?" He looked over at the mutt that was staring at him, its tongue hung out the side of its mouth and it looked like he was grinning. He'd never been much of a pet owner. His kids wanted one but with his frequent trips and Sara running the inn it just seemed a little too much to take on. Of course there was the cost. They weren't cheap.

She stared at him as if he didn't get it. "This is wild country. We get bears, cougars, feral dogs, and occasionally oddball hikers. You should be safe in here but I'll leave a rifle with you. Do you know how to shoot one?"

"Of course." He'd often taken a gun with him when he delivered planes as some of the places he flew into were remote and safety was a must. Beth cautiously took her hands away from his chest, stood up and went over to the kitchen and rummaged through the cupboards. She took out a few bags of jerky and stuffed them into a backpack. She collected a huge coat and flung it over the back of a sofa nearby.

"Are you hungry?" she asked. "I've got soup."

"I need to…"

"Pee?"

He was embarrassed to say it but it was as if she already knew. She crossed the room and stepped into the bedroom and picked up a silver-colored bedpan. "Don't worry, you've used it twice already."

"But…"

"Yeah, you were a little out of it," she said filling in the blanks. "Wasn't easy, that's for sure." She looked back at him. "Trust me, I didn't want to do it either but I wasn't going to have you piss in the bed again."

He didn't know what to make of that. It was hard to remember in the haze of strong painkillers. He peppered her with more questions about her father, the distance to town nearby and how long she'd been living there. The questions were asked more out of embarrassment than because he was interested. He did the same when he visited his local doctor. While it didn't change the situation it made him feel less self-conscious, however, that was his doctor, a man, an adult. This was a young girl. Somehow though she managed to help him keep his dignity. Beth put on disposable gloves, and rolled him on his side which made him cry out in pain. Next she placed the bedpan against his buttocks and rolled him back over.

"Where did you learn to do this?"

"My mother was a nurse," she replied as she took away the urine-filled bedpan and emptied it outside.

The door slammed shut and for a few seconds he was alone barring the dog who just kept staring at him. "Shoo. Go," he said feeling as if the dog was peering into his very soul.

Beth returned, glanced at the dog and at him. "You'll get used to him."

Used to him? She made it sound like he was going to be there a long time. He wasn't. As soon as he could stand, he would make his way home, one way or another. Beth went over to the kitchen and returned with a large thermos.

"Here, it's soup." She perched on the edge of the bed and unscrewed the top which was a cup. She poured some out and brought it to his lips, lifting his body ever so slightly. He took a sip. It was wasn't hot but warm enough to swallow in one go. It tasted of chicken. "Homemade. Made it myself. There should be enough in there for lunch and dinner though I expect to be back before nightfall."

"Beth."

"I have to go," she said getting up and returning a moment later with a pill container. "Take two every four hours. No more. Okay? They're pretty strong so you'll probably sleep. Before you know it, I'll be back."

Beth shrugged into her coat in preparation to leave, she then crouched near her dog and whispered something into its ear. The dog looked over at him as if it understood. She patted it on the back and slung her backpack on, then collected a .22 lever-action rifle and placed it beside the bed along with a box of ammo. "You familiar with this?"

When he didn't answer her instantly, she showed him how to load it. Once done she looked around the room, biting down gently on her lower lip as if troubled that she'd forgotten something before she palmed a magazine into the P320 and holstered it at her hip. She then collected a bow and quiver, slung it over her shoulder and tucked a small hatchet into the belt around her hip. "Oh, there's bottled water just below the bed. You think you can reach it?" He let his arm hang down and touched it.

"Good. Well, I'll be back soon." She went across the room and tossed a few more logs into the fire, covered it with the protector, smiled and went to exit.

"Beth."

"Yeah?"

"Thank you."

She shrugged as if it was nothing. "Not a problem. Stay warm."

She flung the door open. The sight of bright white snow was blinding. "Beth. Where's your mother?"

Still holding the door she looked back at him for a second before covering her head with a hood. "Dead."

* * *

Slowly she backed away from the cabin and stood in the snow that measured up to her knees. The weather had vastly improved over the past few days. It was clear except for a few flurries. Beth had a basic idea of where the start of the trail was and now the blizzard had passed, she had no doubt she could make it into town within the hour. She didn't like leaving a stranger at the cabin or with her dog but it wasn't like he was a problem. She had a rough idea of where the plane had gone down and would search for his daughter but she knew after twenty-four hours there was no way in hell his kid was alive. Mountain weather could be brutal in the winter and after the storm they'd just been through, and with the number of wild animals out looking for food, the odds of finding her body would be slim to none.

Time was against her. There was no telling if another storm would sweep in and she didn't want to be hiking in the dark. Her first priority was to make it to town, head to the outdoor center and see if she could locate her father. Next, she would head over to the home of Gregory Banks, an elderly doctor who worked in a small clinic in town. He'd been a close friend of the family from way back when her mother used to commute to Cannon Memorial Hospital which was the nearest hospital, located a thirty-minute drive away from town.

Beth gazed up into the deep blue sky as birds squawked overhead.

Her feet plunged into the fresh powder as she trudged forward. It would take a good thirty minutes of hard slogging through the forest and another ten to reach the town by road and that was if she picked up the pace. She made a beeline for the mouth of the trail, picking up her feet and panting hard.

Within minutes her thighs burned and sweat trickled from her brow.

She kept pressing on through the high drifts of untouched snow. Ten minutes passed and she kept her eyes out for the wreckage. She passed birds feasting on something. She shooed them away hoping it wasn't Landon's daughter. It wasn't. It was a torn-up rabbit. It was like hiking through a maze, pines everywhere she turned blocking her view. It would have been easy for someone who didn't know these mountains to lose their footing and break an ankle. The rough terrain challenged hikers. Continuing on, she crested a rise and saw the familiar distant sight of Ryerson in the valley. Why hadn't she seen the lights last night? And why was there black smoke drifting over the buildings?

Beth hurried, concern spreading on her face. Something wasn't right.

Several times she nearly lost her footing and had to reach out and brace herself against a tree. As she picked up speed and her boots disappeared below, snow piled through the small opening around each boot, and soaked her jeans.

Still, she didn't even think about that, her mind stayed on the sight of smoke — that was until she reached the mountain road. It was unplowed. How could that be? It was always plowed. Locals, and visitors trying to head west, relied upon that road. It was completely untouched barring abandoned vehicles. It was the strangest sight.

She walked past one, two, six vehicles on the way in.

No one was inside.

One even had the doors left wide open and looked as if it had been rifled through.

Beth hurried towards the cluster of buildings that made up Ryerson, questions bombarding her mind, panic rising in her chest. Snow-covered from head to toe, her lungs burned as she ran. Up ahead smoke rose into the chilly air coming from not one but several buildings that had been burned to the ground. She could see what looked like the burned-out steel bones of a Toyota sedan that had gone through a storefront. There had been a collision between two vehicles, with one of them turned on its side.

Her father's workplace was west on the outskirts of town, requiring her to cut through. With her stomach in her throat from running so hard, she slowed; taking in the sights and trying to catch her breath. Vehicles clogged up the two lanes of Main Street which wound its way into the heart of town. Many of the residents were out clearing the sidewalk of snow, others trying to push vehicles that had collided out of the way, while others talked among themselves. Beth avoided the crowds but listened to the conversations as she passed: *No my phone is still not working. What would cause the cars to stall?* They all shared the same pained expression. It was like something out of a bizarre horror movie. What had happened?

Chapter 12

The closer Beth got to the Outdoor Education Center, the more abandoned vehicles she found encased in snow. No roads had been plowed, making the journey even more of a slog and a challenge. Eagles Nest, which was the name of her father's center, was created nine years ago after generous donations. It had allowed her father to purchase a property on 200 acres of land, five minutes outside of Ryerson in the Pisgah National Forest. At the end of an off-the-beaten path was a collection of eight cabins offering lodging and activities for young people from kindergarten age through to twelfth grade. Her father Rhett had the dream to learn and teach in the mountains since he was a boy. He'd seen the abuse of resources and the way nature had been neglected and children raised in a world of technology. His passion to explore new valleys, climb ridges, paddle rivers, feel the rain on his face and experience plants and animals had led him to build the center. And, for the most part it had been a success.

Beth had spent many a summer helping her father at the center while her mother worked outside of town. It was where she'd cut her teeth in the wilderness, learned responsibility and gained valuable leadership qualities.

Tired, cold and hungry, she saw the familiar sign buried below snow. She didn't need to see the words to know what they said: *Respect yourself, others, and the natural world.* It was a motto that drove him to spend days, weeks and months with campers.

"You better have a good excuse," she said, expecting to find him wallowing in self-pity, surrounded by bottles of alcohol. For all his strengths, the death of her mother had blindsided him. He didn't expect it, nor did Beth. The manner in which it happened went contrary to her choice of career and view of the world. Two years later, Beth still wrestled with it. It seemed like such a waste of a life. She learned a lot about her mother after that, things that her father didn't share and things her mother had hid from her.

Towering drifts of snow sent a frigid windblown spray at her face as she got near. Beth pulled at her hood, kept her head low and pressed into the clearing. "Dad!" she hollered, her voice disappearing in the vastness of forest. In the summer it would have been packed with kids dressed in colorful T-shirts and shorts, running from lodge to lodge, or hanging out at the snack bar or taking in one of the workshops or hiking trails and rivers. Now it was empty and silent. Nothing but white. The ATV wasn't parked outside which concerned her. Had he even made it here? Or was he at a bar in town?

Her worst fear was he'd had an accident.

That question was soon answered when she found the front door ajar and a large snowdrift blown through. The wind howled. There was no way he would leave the place unlocked. There was no damage to the property which meant no one had broken in.

"Dad?" her voice echoed as she entered the dark octagon-shaped log cabin that was used for sleeping, administration and a central hub for campers. The familiar scent of pine brought with it memories. With just a year left until she went off to college, she was going to miss helping out in the summer as a staff member. Beth noticed the door to the main office was open. Papers were scattered over the floor. Had the wind done that? She called out to her father but got no response. It was only when she stepped inside that she saw a chair turned over, and a pair of female legs.

Instinctively her hand reached for the P320, taking it out and moving in.

As Beth came around the office counter, Helen's body came into view.

"Helen."

She was in her mid-fifties, a hard-working woman, single, no kids. She had been one of a few that had volunteered her time to the center long before her father was able to pay. Beth dropped down, touching her skin. It was icy cold. There was a deep, red and purple mark around her throat which indicated strangulation.

Fear.

She hadn't felt anything that came that close.

Beth had faced close calls with cougars and bears but this was on another level.

This was impossible. No. It couldn't be. Denial hit her hard. Ryerson was a safe community. Residents had each other's backs. Who would have done this? Most in town knew about the center. She staggered back from the body wanting to cry out her fathers name but words stuck in her throat. Were they still here? No. There were no tracks in the snow. This had been done in the storm. Beth raced out, calling for her father while keeping her gun out in front of her. "Dad!" She hurried down the corridor that led into an open space where campers would have breakfast.

Beth froze at the familiar sight of her father's jacket.

"No. No. NO!" she screamed rushing forward, dropping to her knees beside her father's motionless body that was face down. There were two bullet wounds to the back. His face was swollen, bruised, as were his knuckles as if he'd put up one hell of a fight.

"Dad. Dad!" she cried out, grasping a clump of his jacket and burying her face in it.

* * *

Beth wasn't sure how long she remained there but it had to have been over an hour, two maybe. She had all but drained her inner well of tears before she lifted her head. Losing her mother was hard enough at her age but now her father? She sat across from him, staring, unsure of what to do, if anything at all. What now? Her entire world had revolved around her parents. She ran a hand over her face wanting to cry again but was unable to. All she felt was numb. Complete numbness.

She got up and left the room and searched for a blanket, sheet, tarp, anything she could use to cover their bodies. Once done, she went throughout the property and noticed that the three ATVs they owned were gone including the one her father used. In addition to this the storage room that held food had been cleared out. Every shelf including bottled water had been taken. She moved on to the next room that had climbing gear, tents, tarps, sleeping bags, water treatments, stoves, lighting, first aid, clothing, electronics and backpacks, it was all gone. Her father had poured his money into purchasing lots of gear so that anyone who didn't have enough money didn't go without.

Was this a robbery gone wrong?

The Christmas season was the only time of the year when her father and Helen were alone at the property. Had someone targeted it? Or were they an opportunist? No, it had to be something more. Her father would have gladly handed it all over to avoid a confrontation. He believed in staying alive, not fighting over items that could be replaced.

But what other reason would they have been killed?

Without answers, Beth did the only thing she could: leave and head back to town to inform the police. Like traveling the same road to work unconsciously and arriving at a destination without recollection of having driven there, Beth found herself standing outside the

Ryerson Police Department with no memory of walking there. She entered the stone and wood building with an American flag flapping in the breeze to find concerned residents speaking to an officer at the front desk. They were grossly understaffed to handle something of this magnitude.

"Vehicles. Internet. Power. Water. Cell phones. Nothing is working. I want to know what is being done?" an angry man yelled, slamming his fist against the counter.

"Sir, we know about as much as you do right now. As you can appreciate, with the weather we've been having and cruisers not working, our top priority right now is ensuring the safety of residents."

She could have said something. Dropped the bombshell about her father being dead but she didn't. So overwhelmed by grief and shock, she stood at the back of the lobby watching as if in some trance state. Ahead of her was a long line of people wanting answers.

"Is it a terrorist attack?"

"Ma'am. I don't know."

"And what about power? My mother could die from this cold," a woman yelled.

"We're doing the best we can to speak to the utility company but until we have some answers all we can do is apologize and ask you to go home."

"Go home. Go home!?" A young man in a plaid shirt shoved his way to the front. "That's not good enough. There are people relying on this power to survive. We need a generator."

"I believe you can still buy one."

"With what?"

"Cash works," the officer said.

"Oh yeah, I just have an extra thousand dollars sitting around for days like this. No. The city should be rolling out some kind of emergency plan."

"And you will be the first to hear about it," the officer said.

Beth didn't stand a chance at being heard. The uproar from the twenty-odd people crammed into the lobby was deafening. Questions were thrown out, voices raised and each one was thinking their situation mattered more. Beth lowered her chin and walked back out and sat down on the snow-covered step even as a cold blast of wind chilled her to the bone. She didn't care. While she was waiting there, out the corner of her eye she saw a female officer shrugging on a winter jacket from the back of her cruiser. She looked over at Beth and squinted. "Is that you, Beth?"

She didn't respond.

The female officer strolled over adjusting her duty belt looking as if she was getting ready to start a shift. Her hair was pulled up into a severe black ponytail. As she got closer, Beth recognized her as someone who'd dropped off her kid at the outdoor center. Her name was Sylvia Robson. "What are you doing here?" she asked before glancing through the glass doors at the mob. "Rhett inside?"

She shook her head trying to summon the words to tell her but they wouldn't come out. Maybe it was because she didn't want to believe it, or perhaps saying it would make it final. "You okay, Beth?"

Tears welled in her eyes as Sylvia crouched in front of her placing both hands on her knees. "Hey. Hey, what's up?"

"He's gone."

"Who's gone?"

"He's dead."

"Beth. Who?"

"My father."

Silence followed.

Her words registered.

"Rhett is dead?"

And just like that it all spilled out, everything she'd seen. The officer gripped her shoulder. "Look, honey, there's a trailer around back that's heated by a generator. Why don't you go and sit in there while I look into this. Just tell them I sent you." Beth nodded and followed a short path around the back of the department to a single-wide 12 x 60 trailer; the type often seen on construction sites. With the power down, they'd set up a facility to operate out of that would be easier to heat than the main building. No wonder the officer inside at the front desk was dressed in a heavy coat, beanie and gloves. She ascended the steel steps and entered one of the two brown doors. Inside, a wall of warmth greeted her as did a male officer by the name of Tim Sturgeon. "Can I help you?"

"Officer Robson asked me to wait."

"Sure. Take a seat."

She sat down and watched four officers talk among themselves. They had a large map on the wall of Ryerson and the surrounding areas, and one of them was pushing in colored pins and discussing a plan of action.

While she sat there her mind shifted to Landon. A hand rose to her forehead. *Oh no.* In all the chaos she'd almost forgotten him. She couldn't have another death on her conscience. Beth got up and walked out without giving them a statement. "Hey kid," a cop said as the door swung shut and she bolted; heading for the one person that might be able to help.

* * *

Dr. Gregory Banks had invited her mother and father for dinner on two occasions. He owned a gorgeous five-bedroom home nestled on over seven acres of property, on a knoll buried amid the lush forest. Beth could remember entering the home and looking up at the soaring ceilings, floating staircase, granite countertops, high-end appliances and being surrounding by an abundance of glass that let in natural light. It was a million-dollar home, a mixture of stone and wood that he'd had custom built for his family. Unlike her father, her mother thought such things mattered. Beth recalled the uncomfortable conversation around the table that night. Her father looked like a fish out of water whereas her mother was in her element. The differences between the two of them were so stark that she often wondered how they ever stayed together. Her mother worked a regular job thirty minutes outside of Ryerson, and was interested in the finer things in life, and her father's passion was the outdoors. Somehow, they managed to merge the two and compromise.

It took her twenty minutes to reach his home.

She figured he'd be at the medical center or offering his services at the hospital in Linville but as she got closer, she saw him beyond the glass. His expression brightened at the sight of her then faded as he opened the door.

"Beth. What are you doing here?"

"I need your help."

Chapter 13

It was beyond strange. Stalled vehicles clogged the main arteries in and out of towns and hamlets; fires burned out of control and everyday electronic devices no longer seemed to work. Russ thought he was trapped in an episode of *The Twilight Zone* or having a vivid nightmare.

After killing the cops and relieving them of their weapons, they'd circled around Maggie Valley due to the commercial airliner that had torn through the town turning Main Street into a blazing inferno. The hike to Ryerson would have taken roughly forty hours had they not hijacked a blue 1971 Beetle in the early hours of the second morning. Like many other curious onlookers, Russ couldn't believe his eyes when he heard the roar of an engine, and saw it slaloming around stalled vehicles on US-19E.

Of course the driver had no intention of stopping as

they watched the Beetle veer around a family that tried to flag them down for help.

Survival. It was all about staying alive. Every man for himself.

Having already witnessed the death of three police officers, he didn't bat an eye to Tommy's suggestion to open fire on it. They didn't stop to discuss morals. No, instead the three of them stood in the middle of the road, equally spaced out, Glocks raised and ready to unleash hell. They aimed for the windshield to avoid damaging the engine. People moving along the road stepped back in horror as rounds shattered the glass, a mist of red sprayed and the driver lost control and coasted to a standstill only a stone's throw away.

Acting fast, they dragged the driver out and hopped in, tearing away.

He remembered looking back in the rearview mirror and seeing a crowd gather around the driver's body and looking at them. What were they gonna do? Cell phones didn't work. Cop cars were nowhere to be seen and even if they were nearby, they weren't functioning.

So why was this car working? The only thing they could conclude was that it was built on really old technology, a motor that didn't have a hint of electronics. At least that's what Tommy said, that kid considered himself an expert on vehicles, and anything else for that matter, but that was debatable otherwise he wouldn't have dropped out of college.

Before stealing the vehicle, the highway that night had been cluttered with people going both ways. Some asked them if they knew what had happened, as if they had the answers or could reveal a fragment of the puzzle. But he had no idea. He didn't expect anyone else did unless they were individuals linked to the event, like government, military or some expert. The average joe? Please. When people weren't working as a slave in a nine-to-five job they had their nose buried in a movie, a book or social media. That was reality for the largest percentage of the population. They would have seen the media cover wildfires, floods, tornadoes, and storms that knock out power, but those were common disasters, events that America had bounced back from time and time again. But this? This made no sense. Seeing people walking along the road, cars broken down, planes dropping out of the sky, multiple crashes, buildings on fire with smoke rising was strange — not even terrorists were smart enough to coordinate an attack of this magnitude. They'd had this discussion on the way home. If terrorists were planning to strike, they would target large cities or military installations, key areas that would hamstring the country or garner international attention, not small towns in America. Especially not North Carolina. There was no reason, no incentive. At least not one he could see.

They arrived in Ryerson sometime after eight, expecting to see the town in flames but besides a couple of buildings the damage was minimal. They quickly made a beeline for Cayden's business on the north side. Cayden Harrington ran a bar called Harrington's. It was nothing more than a façade that covered his illegal operations; the main source of income came from drug distribution. He was the go-to guy for drugs for many in four counties. A smart individual, he never got his hands dirty and always let others do the grunt work. As they swerved the Beetle around the back of the bar, Russ noticed four guys unloading survival gear into a garage and rolling a collection of ATVs off the back of three old beat-up trucks. He always had his hands in a variety of things but that was strange even for him. The ATVs would be of no use to him now. Had they worked they wouldn't have carjacked that Beetle. Cayden was outside giving directions. He glanced their way and cupped a hand over his eyes to block the glare of sunlight.

Cayden was an imposing man, close to six foot with a fierce beard, and military buzz cut. Some said he'd been a Marine at one time but others dispelled those rumors as nothing more than hot air from a man trying to inflate his ego. Cayden relished the mystique around him and had always fancied himself as some kind of Godfather figure.

Growing up Russ had looked up to his uncle, admired the way he'd walk into a room and be treated with respect. He had this wicked tattoo of a lion on his neck that stretched down beneath his shirt, and he always wore a flat gray cap. Today he was wearing a dark navy peacoat, tight jeans and black boots.

"Let me do the talking," Russ said looking over at Morgan who had a tendency to put his foot in his mouth. They got out and Cayden made his way over but not before bellowing out a few more orders.

"Throw some tarps over the ATVs and get them inside." He turned towards Russ and extended his hand like he often did, bringing him in for a pat on the back. "What have we got here?" he said admiring the Beetle.

"Picked it up on the way through. Not many vehicles out there working."

"Tell me about it," he said. "I don't know what the hell is happening but we press on, business as usual. So. How did it go? You collect the goods?"

He sucked his bottom lip in and looked over at the others. "That's the thing."

"Russ."

"The plane went down. We were there but that's when the lights went out."

"So you followed it and collected my shit?"

"No."

"What do you mean no?"

"Cayden. Look around you. There's no power. Vehicles aren't working. The roads are clogged with people. Buildings are on fire."

"And business will continue," he said as if none of that mattered. "This is just a glitch. What, you think I'm closing down?" He turned towards the garage. "You see all that? That's so business can continue even while this shitstorm is being dealt with."

"But what if it's not?"

"Not what?"

"Being dealt with."

He laughed and put a hand around his neck and pulled him forcefully away from the others. "Please tell me you saw where that plane went down?"

"It went past us and disappeared somewhere in the

Pisgah National Forest."

"Then why the hell are you here?"

"What?"

"You should be out there looking for it."

Russ looked back at him, mouth agape. "Cayden, first, we have no idea where it could be and second, even if we did know, your cocaine is probably scattered all over the mountain."

Cayden led him out of view of the others and threw him up against a wall, then wrapped his hand around his neck and began squeezing while attempting to lift him off the ground. "For your sake that better not be true."

"Uncle. Please," he spluttered, hoping to snap him out of his deranged state.

Cayden released him and placed a hand on his shoulder. "I want you to find that plane."

"But with the storm. It could be anywhere."

"Then I guess you'll be busy for the next few weeks."

He couldn't believe what he was asking.

"But how? Where do we begin? The forest has

thousands of acres."

Tommy and Morgan walked around the corner; they'd been eavesdropping. Like a concerned friend, or just trying to impress Cayden, Morgan threw in his two cents. "I think I know how we can find it."

Cayden gave him a stern look. "How?"

"You gave Dustin a personal locator beacon, right? Just in case he had to come down in a different area or just in case things got hot and he had to cut off communication."

Russ knew where he was going with this but it was pointless.

"It won't work," Russ muttered. "In theory it's a good idea but all electronics have stopped and besides, those things only have a 30-hour battery runtime. It's been far longer than that," Russ said as he rubbed his red neck.

Cayden jumped in. "I don't give a shit. You had one job and that was to collect the drop, you still haven't done that so I want you to get out there and find it."

"But uncle. You don't understand."

He shouldn't have said that. Cayden threw a punch into his gut, his legs buckled and he dropped to the ground. "No, you don't understand. I want my twenty keys."

"I have a rough idea where the plane went down," Tommy piped up, trying to come to his aid. Cayden looked at him unconvinced after what Morgan said.

"Oh yeah? How?"

Tommy continued. "It's simple math. Based on our location, altitude, speed, and the direction it was heading. I might not get an exact location of the crash but I can figure it out. I just need a map."

Now had it been anyone else, Cayden might have called bullshit on it but Tommy was generally considered an intelligent man even though he'd dropped out of college. He could see Cayden chewing it over. He released his grip on Russ and backed up. "Then why are you standing around? Get to it!" he said walking away from them. Tommy crouched and helped Russ up.

"You okay, man?"

Russ nodded, trying not to show weakness but his neck burned, his stomach was doing flips. Tommy offered to carry him back to the Beetle but he chose to walk by himself.

"And Tommy!" Cayden called out. "Once you have a location. You let me know. I'm going with you to make sure you guys don't fuck it up again."

Great. That was all he needed. Now he definitely couldn't skim off the top. As they backed out and headed for Tommy's house, Russ began to have his doubts. "Listen, I appreciate what you did back there but there is no way we'll find that plane. It's like looking for a needle in a haystack. And with everything that's happened, perhaps this is the time to part ways."

"As much as I wanted to help, I wasn't lying. I think we can find it. It won't be easy but... I have a few ideas."

"Like?"

"The map obviously. I think I can figure out the trajectory. But the other is asking around town, checking in with the medical center. There is a slim chance Dustin survived and if he did maybe he made his way down or was brought in. We can ask."

Russ brought a hand up to his face and squeezed the bridge of his nose as he drove out of the lot. He could feel a migraine coming on, probably from a lack of sleep over the past two days but it was also stress. He'd seen what Cayden had done to those who screwed him over and although he was his nephew, he knew he wouldn't give him leniency.

"So basically you don't know," Morgan said from the backseat before chuckling. "Great. Looks like you're screwed, Russ."

Russ slammed the brakes on and twisted in his seat. "You think I'm the only one that will go down for this if we don't find that coke?" Morgan stared back dumbfounded. "You can be such a moron at times." He hit the accelerator and continued on. It didn't take long to arrive at Tommy's home. It was an apartment on the west side not far from the medical center. He lived alone, choosing to date women rather than settle down. While him and Morgan didn't have a future because they lacked an education and only knew a life of crime, Tommy knew shit. That was the best way to put it. He was smart but had chosen to bail after going through a bad relationship with some girl. He said it had done him in, and made it too difficult to concentrate on work.

As they got out and entered his two-story aluminum-sided home, they were greeted by three cats that came bounding towards them. Morgan turned up his nose. "It smells like cat piss in here. Seriously, open a window."

Tommy took them into a modest kitchen. He kept his place clean but with three cats it was hard to control smell. Tommy quickly emptied out a cat litter tray into a bag and tossed it in the backyard. Then he went into another room and returned with a yellow marker and a map. "Give me a hand clearing off the table," he said. Russ removed a bowl, a cup and a money tree plant then Tommy laid down the map and smoothed it out.

He couldn't believe he was serious about this.

"I thought you were joking?" Russ said.

"No. Why would I do that?"

"Uh maybe because Pisgah is over 500,000 acres!"

Tommy waved at him and continued on unfazed. "Okay, here's where we were," he said drawing a large yellow circle around Ghost Town in the Sky theme park. He jotted down a few numbers, and what appeared to be an estimate of the height and speed, then he drew an X in a location west. "This was the direction I saw the plane heading in. Now think about it. Dustin was a bush pilot. He was used to setting that thing down in remote locations. He would have tried to bring it down in an area that was open. Now I think he went down around…"

"Hold it right there, Tommy. I think you're overlooking something important."

"Which is?"

"The lights went out which means the ground would have looked like the sky, pitch black. There would have been no visual cue to determine where to land, and without instruments to tell him how high he was, he could have gone…" He took the pen from Tommy and circled it around a section of the forest that went from Pensacola to Blowing Rock. "There. He could have gone down anywhere inside of there. Now you understand what I was trying to say," he said tossing the pen on the table and walking away. As much as he admired his friend's determination and respected his intelligence, this was a crapshoot, nothing more than a guessing game. It was too difficult to figure out accurately where the plane might have crashed unless they were nearby when it came down. Besides they were distracted by the Boeing that crashed within minutes after the lights went out.

"So what do you want to do?" Tommy said.

Russ turned to him. "I say we get the fuck out of here. Leave Ryerson."

"This is my home. I'm not leaving," Morgan said.

"Then you'll die. Cayden doesn't give a shit about you, me or anyone but himself. He knows we can't find it. He's delaying the inevitable."

Tommy stepped forward. "Well I say we at least pay the medical center a visit. See if Dustin did make it.

That's if he even made it this far."

To stick around was absurd but until they knew what was happening in town venturing beyond the town limits would have been equally absurd.

Chapter 14

The unknown. Sara had never been very good at dealing with it. Landon could handle it, not her. And now her worst fear was getting the better of her. What if the plane Hank saw go down had been them? No, don't go there, she thought. She shivered in Jake's 1979 Scout on the way back from Hancock County Bar Harbor Airport in Trenton. He'd offered to take her out there to see if they'd arrived but the airport was closed. It felt like a complete waste of time and gas. She'd apologized three times in the space of half an hour, offering gas money but Jake told her to relax and keep it. The heater was on full blast but with 21 degrees outside, it was doing little to keep them warm. She peered through the frosted windshield; her mind lost. Jake tried to stay positive.

"I'm sure there's a good reason. Landon might still be in Alabama."

"No, I got his message on the voice mail. He was on

his way back," she said.

Jake nodded and kept looking ahead. A few times in the trip there and back groups of people had tried to flag them down seeking a ride but Jake wouldn't slow which seemed odd to her. On the fourth time they passed a group she spoke up. "You know there is room in the back."

"It's too dangerous," he said.

"Why?"

He sucked in a breath and cast a sideways glance at her. "Minimal vehicles are on the road. It makes people like us a target."

She laughed. "Are you serious?"

"Of course."

"This is Maine, Jake, not New York City."

"That's being a little biased," he said.

She smirked. "No I'm just saying; people are generally friendly."

"When things are going well. This is affecting the whole country, Sara. You saw those downed planes, those buildings on fire in Ellsworth. We are dealing with a completely different beast."

"Okay, I will admit it's strange but…"

"It's not strange. It's an EMP."

"A what?"

"You've never heard of that before?"

"Why would I? I get up early, spend my days catering to guests and by the end of the day I am too damn tired to be browsing online researching EMTs."

"EMP," he said correcting her with a chuckle.

She pulled a face. "All right, smart-ass. I'm just saying, I'm lucky if I can get some free time to take a bath."

"I don't know, you smell good to me," he replied in a flirtatious manner.

She slapped him on the arm and went slightly red in the face.

He nodded. "Anyway, sounds like you need to slow down."

"What, like you?" she asked, casting a glance at him knowing full well he worked all the hours under the sun.

"Touché," he replied, his mouth cracking into a smile.

She groaned. "Ugh, what's happened to us? It's like my entire life revolves around making ends meet. I never envisioned this when I was a kid. Life seemed so much more..." she searched for the words.

"Lighter?" Jake asked.

"Yeah," she nodded. "Lighter. Carefree. Now it's all about paying bills, staying ahead of the tax man and arguing."

"Arguing?"

She realized she'd put her foot in her mouth. "Um..." At one time she and Landon never argued. It was a joy to be around him but over the past few years it seemed like all the fun had been sucked out of the relationship. It felt more like work than something that flowed naturally. They were always butting up against each other, arguing about small, stupid, insignificant things that later she would shake her head at. She loved him — dearly — but with him delivering planes all the time and her focused on the inn she would have been lying to say that they hadn't grown apart. The ember that once glowed bright and brought them to life had all but fizzled out. When he was home, he wasn't there. His mind was elsewhere and she expected him to chip in and help around the manor but all he wanted to do was relax, go fishing or sit out in the yard. It was like they were worlds apart. Obviously, she didn't hound him and maybe it was because she was working all hours of the day and night that she figured he should too. It was hard to separate the business from the home.

Sara quickly changed the subject rather than drag him down into the mire of her shaky marriage. "So this EMP… How could it happen? What is it? And how long does it last?" She peppered him with questions and he did his best to bring her up to speed on what he'd learned from a client who'd brought in an old Jeep.

"Look, I can only relay what I was told by this client. I mean I laughed the first time he told me that he'd bought this banged-up old Jeep in preparation for some apocalyptic event but it got me thinking. I looked into it and the next thing I knew I snapped up this Scout at an auction for next to nothing. Figured it would sit in my garage gathering dust and I'd never use it. Lo and behold, here we are," he said. "It seems there's a lot of confusion in the general public about EMPs, what they are, how they happen and what they affect. I won't bore you with it."

"Well I think I should at least know what we're dealing with."

He groaned. "Electro-magnetic pulse or EMP for short. Believe me, there are some headcases out there who really get riled up about this stuff as if they have something to prove. But the short explanation is it can come from a nuclear missile detonating or a coronal mass ejection."

"A what?" She was getting more confused by the minute.

"A solar flare. From the sun. Often called a CME. Again there is a lot of confusion surrounding it, but basically in a nutshell an EMP is broken into three component pulses. An E1 is brief, fast and intense. This is basically why our computers and communication aren't functioning. It damages the electrical elements. You then have an E2 which tends to occur in lightning strikes, our nation is somewhat prepared to handle that. Then you have an E3 which is slower, similar to a geomagnetic storm that comes from a solar flare. This can damage power lines, transformers and so forth. Basically any critical infrastructure. Some will argue that a CME doesn't include an E1 or an E2 and so the only things that would be affected would be the power grid, not vehicles or smaller electronics, so they tend to refer to it as a solar EMP and not an EMP by itself. Anyway, if I had to put money on it, my best guess is this is nuclear not a solar event, or... maybe it's a combination."

As he rattled on, it just went right over her head. "Yeah, this is probably why I don't look into this," Sara said.

He laughed. "Not exactly stuff you listen to as you're dozing off at night," he said. "Look, all you need to know is we're screwed. That's the bottom line." He said it in such a nonchalant way.

"Hold on a minute. But I thought we were looking at a few days, maybe a week or two at most. That's how things went in the last snowstorm."

"Sara, a snowstorm didn't cause this. We've just happened to have one at the same time. Lucky us, I guess," he said. "No, what I'm talking about here is no electricity, no internet, no communication, no transportation, no deliveries, no water, no food. Do the math. Society will soon unravel. Maybe not today or next week but eventually. You don't bounce back from this easily."

There was silence in the Scout except for the sound of tires crunching over snow.

"But the landlines work," she said.

"Yeah, when people have the old ones. Ones that don't rely on external power. Cordless models or any phone that relies on AC power are of no use. You, Janice, Hank just happen to have the old style. You specifically have the previous owners of that nineteenth century home to thank for that. Hell, I'm surprised you didn't change it over."

"We were planning on getting rid of them and going strictly to cell phones."

"Anyway, just because you have one, that doesn't mean someone else does. Most of society today have ditched landlines for modern phones."

"So how long will mine work?"

"As long as there is backup power at the central office. Once that stops working, we'll have to go back to message boards. Have some central message board in town and use handwritten messages."

"Are you serious?" She laughed unable to grasp the gravity of the situation. How could she? They'd never experienced this before.

"You have a ham radio?"

"No. Do you?"

He shook his head. "No."

"And yet you bought a 1979 Scout to avoid an

apocalyptic event?"

"What can I say? It was an auction, a bargain."

Both of them laughed as they drove south on ME-166. However, Sara's laughter soon faded at the seriousness of the event. What did this mean? How would they survive?

"What about FEMA?"

Jake sighed. "I like to think positively, Sara, but everything about this is pointing to an event I don't think we'll come back from, in which case, I'm sure camps will appear but they'll probably start in the big cities and work their way out from there. My concern is surviving the now."

"And how do we do that?" He didn't answer immediately. She knew that whatever time he'd given to learn about such an event would have been minimal so she didn't have high expectations, but at least it gave her some comfort to know that someone recognized the warning signs. Maybe they could use that to their advantage.

"How much food and water do you have?"

"Um," she tried to think. "A pantry that we have for guests and some items for Christmas but it's dwindled a lot. Usually we do a big shop nearer the end of February and stock up then in preparation for March's guests. As for water. I told Max to fill the tubs and sinks and we have some cases of bottled water but that's it."

"And money?" She wasn't too sure she wanted to share that information with him. Then again maybe he already knew since he arrived that morning when she was holding five hundred.

"Sara?" he asked again.

"Roughly five hundred."

"Roughly?"

"I mean on hand. Yeah."

"Good. You'll need that. When we get back you need to stock up. Right now most are notching this up to the storm, thinking it will last a week at most. Once people get word of what's really happening, shit's gonna get really bad in town. The stores, the pharmacies, gas stations, all of it will be wiped out whether that be through people buying with cash or looting."

"Looting? You make it sound like…"

"Do you have a gun?"

Everything that came out of his mouth was throwing her off.

"Sara. Do you have a gun?" he repeated himself.

"Landon has a rifle."

"And you know how to fire it?"

"Jake, you're beginning to worry me. Just slow down. For all we know there might be a very good explanation for this."

"A power outage, yeah, I'm with you on that. Planes falling out of the sky? Ninety-five percent of vehicles no longer working? C'mon, Sara, you can't be that naive."

Her brow furrowed. Had Landon said that to her she would have gone at him, and it would have ended in a big argument. Silence stretched between them and then Jake apologized. "I'm sorry."

"It's okay."

"No it's not, I shouldn't assume."

She shrugged. "So I blow five hundred dollars on food and water. What's the worst that can happen, right?"

He nodded and smiled. "Right."

They continued on driving the last stretch of the journey home along Castine Road that was parallel to Penobscot Bay and the town of Penobscot. "You think we can swing by my mother's on the way back? I want her to be with us at the house."

"Yeah, sure, no problem." They veered around stalled vehicles. The roads in their neck of the woods were barren as the weather was too cold to be walking. She was out of her mind with worry about her mother. The low temperatures, her mother's memory not being that great… she was concerned for her welfare. "Jake. Don't you think the town needs to know?"

"They will."

"No, I mean soon."

"Sara. I'm all for sounding the alarm bell but take how you took the news. You think everyone will believe a tow guy? Besides even if they did, all hell will break loose after that. No, we need to keep this between us until we have your mother, and we've stocked up on food and water."

"What happens when the water runs out?"

"Rivers, streams, collecting rainwater then purifying it."

As they pulled up outside her mother's home, Jake said he would wait outside as he didn't want to leave the Scout. "Just make it quick, okay?"

She nodded and hurried into the house, letting herself in with her key. As soon as she walked in, she noticed how cold it was. Her breath formed in front of her mouth like she was outside. "Mom. Mom?" There was no answer. She went into the living room and noticed two of the windows were ajar. She went over and closed them, shivering and still calling for her mother. Sara hurried up the stairs to the next floor and entered her bedroom. "Mom?" Her mother was in bed and looked as if she was asleep, except the color of her skin was deathly pale. Sara walked over and touched her hand; it was like ice. Shock set in, then she cried out in anguish.

Chapter 15

He drifted. The pain rolled over him and then he drifted into oblivion. The radio played lightly in the background and then nothing but static. A grandfather clock ticked and he'd heard it chime multiple times. He tried to keep count of the hours passing but went unconscious between. The dog. That damn dog hadn't taken its eyes off him. Surely it should be gnawing on a bone, curled up into a deep sleep or chasing its tail. No. Like a guard waiting to change shift, it remained stoic, unmoving. What was going through its mind? What if she didn't return? Did anyone else know he was here? Could it smell his blood? Would it gnaw on his legs out of hunger? Strange thoughts played in the theater of his mind as the painkillers wreaked havoc in his system. It was a wicked combination of relief and torture. He'd never been one for taking medication. Sara would literally have to sneak it into food like an owner might with a pet after surgery. It wasn't the bitter taste but the side effects, the stomach pain, the nausea.

Landon propped himself up on his elbow and reached over to take another two pills. He pawed at the side table trying to reach them while avoiding falling out of bed. His fingers clamped around the plastic container and he sank back, clutching them tightly. It was easier to swallow with the soup. At least it masked the flavor.

He swept back his sheets and looked at his deformed legs which were a funky shade of purple and clay. He'd touched the skin, staring at the lumpy shape. Thirty-nine years and he'd never once broken a bone. He'd often wondered what the pain felt like and now he wished he could forget.

After swallowing, Landon lay back, looking at the ceiling, listening to the howling wind of winter. In the hours since Beth left, he'd shivered and sweated, drifting in and out of sleep only to awake with the pain of loss that felt like dull and sharp knives being driven into him over and over again. Tears fell and he wrestled with dark thoughts of self-harm. He'd heard about parents losing their kids but nothing could prepare him for the trauma or the barrage of what-ifs. If he hadn't taken her. If he'd just listened to Sara. If he'd got on that flight the next day, perhaps…

From outside came the first sounds of Beth returning. At least he hoped it was her. Crunching snow. Barely audible conversation. A male voice. Landon snagged up the Winchester and aimed it at the wooden door across the way, expecting the worst. Although she was a stranger, he was helpless without her. It seemed ironic that he found himself relying on someone younger than him when he prided himself on being self-reliant and rarely needing the help of others. Flying to far-flung countries required more than skill, it demanded absolute confidence in one's ability to handle extreme situations alone. And yet here he was at the mercy of a teen.

A droplet of sweat trickled down the side of his face as the door swung open and a ramp of snow blew in followed by Beth and a bundled-up figure carrying a thick, creased brown leather bag in one hand and crutches in the other. The dog scampered over, bouncing around in excitement. "Yes, yes, hello there," she said, grinning before glancing at Landon. He lowered the barrel of the gun. "I brought a doctor with me," she said placing down two steel poles.

The doctor revealed his face as he flung back his hood. "Hello there," he said. "I'm Dr. Gregory Banks. And you must be Landon. You're looking a little worse for wear." The doctor was around five foot eight, a barrel-chested man with a round face, a full head of white hair, and salt-and-pepper beard. He shook off snow from his coat, removed his boots and made his way over. "Beth. I'll need some towels, and hot water. Can you get that?"

She set off to collect the items while he extended a hand. "Well let's take a look at you." He flung back the woolly covers and nodded slowly. "That doesn't look good at all."

"It's broken, right?"

The doctor's brow furrowed. "Oh, it's broken but to what extent is hard to know. Unfortunately we don't have access to an X-ray machine to get a better look which is what we would usually do in situations like this. Getting you down the mountain in this condition would be problematic and liable to cause more harm than good. And even if we could, we only have a generator to run a few items. Most of the electronic equipment is fried at the medical center, and the hospital is a car ride away. No cars. No travel." He touched his legs a few times and Landon jerked back before he pulled back the covers.

"No power? No cars? What are you talking about?"

Gregory looked at him. "You don't know?"

He shook his head, confused.

"Your plane crashed two days ago, yes?"

He nodded.

"There were several other planes that crashed nearby at the same time the power went out. From what I've learned, this has affected the entire country."

"Entire country!" he said, hoisting himself up onto his

elbows only to groan in pain. Gregory encouraged him to sit still. "What the hell happened? Was it a terrorist attack?"

"No clue. The only information released so far has been general at best." He sniffed hard. "You're lucky Beth found you. What brought you this way?" he said reaching over to his brown bag and unclipping it open. He spread it apart and dug around inside and removed a stethoscope.

"I was trying to get home. I live in Maine."

He placed the drum of the stethoscope against his body in various places and asked him to inhale and exhale. The doctor continued to probe him with questions, making small talk. "Beth said you had your daughter with you."

His chin lowered and the doctor registered it and quickly changed the subject as he felt his shoulder and caused him to grimace in pain. He then shone a light in his eyes, checked his ears and got close to his face. "Your shoulder will need some ice and a sling, plenty of painkillers but should improve over the next six weeks with a full recovery in twelve but the legs…" He looked back down. "That will take some time." He sucked in air and got up and went over to the poles on the ground and returned and set them up beside the bed. It was an IV pole. "We need to replace fluids and electrolytes before and after surgery."

Landon gripped him. "Surgery? What? How?"

His mind was bombarded by questions. He wasn't stupid, he didn't expect to lay in bed for a few weeks and everything to be fine but if it was true and there was no electricity, how would they do that?

"My best guess without seeing inside is that you have a broken tibia and fibula, and the other leg has some small fracture as it doesn't look or feel as bad. In these cases we usually X-ray, then depending on the location, complexity and severity of the break — as well as the patient's age and health — determine how to proceed from there. For fibulas it can be as simple as placing the lower leg and ankle in a cast for six to eight weeks to immobilize the bone. However, depending on how severe or complicated the fracture is, patients often have what is known as an ORIF — an open reduction and internal fixation surgery. This is where we insert metal rods or pins into the bone if it requires an internal fix. Alternatively there are external fixes which hold bone fragments in place and allow for alignment."

His eyes widened at the thought of going under the knife.

Gregory continued. "There are different kinds of breaks. Stable, displaced, stress, spiral, comminuted."

"What do I have?"

"I don't have X-ray vision. Hard to tell. Though I think your left leg has probably a stable fracture whereas the other one is probably spiral or comminuted. Either, you need some surgery."

"How long?"

"Recovery is different for everyone. Some heal fast, others slow. General rule of thumb is that it can take three to six months, and with stress fractures around six to eight weeks. But rest is crucial. You try attempting to walk or run before you can, you're looking at longer."

"Three months?" He balked at the news. He couldn't lay around for three months. Sara. Max. They would need him.

"Or longer. Though quite often patients are back up and walking with crutches after seven weeks. Therapy begins around the six-week mark to prevent stiffness in the knee."

He stared at him as if expecting him to give the thumbs-up or laugh but laughter was the farthest thing from his mind. It was another blow, a crack in the armor he once wore.

"I need to go home."

"I expect you do," he replied taking out more items from his bag. "However, you're not going anywhere for at least three months, not until that is healed."

Landon was having difficulty processing it all. A part of him wished he'd died in the crash, at least then he could be with his daughter, at least then he wouldn't have to be tortured every waking hour by the weight of it all.

"There must be times when surgery isn't possible. Money. A person's age or health, or a power outage. What do you do then?" Landon asked, reaching for a glimmer of hope.

"Landon, no matter what decision is made, the bone has to be aligned and immobilized for it to heal properly. Right now it looks as if it's aligned, thanks to Beth's quick thinking, but without an X-ray or opening the leg I can't be one hundred percent positive about the severity. Can wrenching the leg to alignment and immobilizing it with common sticks and sheets lead to a fix? Of course, the vast majority of fractures will heal without the need for surgery. Long before invasive surgeries were performed that's often the way it had to be done. However that did lead to legs being amputated due to infection. And those who were fortunate to avoid infection often ended up with a loss of mobility that was either partial or total. The concern that most physicians have is in regards to internal bleeding."

Landon sighed as Gregory continued to help him understand the gravity of the situation. "There are displaced and non-displaced fractures. Think about it like this. If you hold a chicken drumstick in your hands and you bend it until you hear a faint crack, the outside might look fine and it can feel solid but you know there is a break. That's a non-displaced fracture. The bone can be set fairly easily using nothing more than a cast because that bone can line up. Then on the other end of the spectrum you snap that drumstick. Now you have part of it flapping around. This is displaced and the two parts might not line up so well and might even overlap. Your left leg, I'm guessing is non-displaced but that right one, Landon…" He didn't have to say any more, he understood, but he continued. Gregory inhaled deeply. "The body has this amazing way of healing itself over time but that doesn't mean it will heal properly, and it may lead to disability or discomfort later."

Beth returned with towels in hand and a bowl of warm water. She set them down nearby and stood back looking over Gregory's shoulder. Landon met her gaze. He appreciated everything she was doing but in that moment his pain wasn't just physical, it was so much more and that clouded his judgment.

"Recovery would be faster without surgery, yes?"

Gregory groaned. "You won't be able to hike out of here in a month if that's what you're thinking. Often without surgery it can take longer, seven, maybe eight months. You've got to remember that leg must be immobilized and you need to restrict activity with bed rest. The fastest I've seen someone walking was around the two-month mark and that was with surgery."

"But you said people do recover from this without surgery."

"Not properly, but yes." He tipped his head back and ran a hand over his beard. "Look, I'm a doctor, Landon. Nearly retired but a doctor nevertheless. I'm just relaying what is common today. In the past that was another thing entirely. The ancient Hindus treated fractures with nothing more than bamboo splints and exercise to prevent muscle atrophy while immobilized, similar to the way we deal with dislocated shoulders today. The Greeks used waxes and resins on bandages to create their own form of a cast while using splints so it all stiffened. Arabians used lime from seashells and albumen from egg whites to stiffen and create their bandaged casts. It worked then. Today we can see inside, determine the severity and internally or externally fix it to enable and facilitate healing."

He nodded feeling another wave of pain. "Just cast it," he said.

"Landon. I'll need to put you on antibiotics and give you some stronger painkillers but…"

"Just do it. Please."

He didn't want to go under the surgeon's knife. He figured he would take his chances. He said a bone would heal eventually. In his mind not having his leg cut into had to lead to a faster recovery. As for the rest — disability? Discomfort? How much worse could it be than what he'd been through?

"Landon, I don't recommend it."

"Having a rod inserted into the bone with screws is invasive, and doesn't surgery of that nature require power tools to drill, cut or screw in? We don't have power and there is still the chance of me getting an infection. The skin isn't broken, doc. It's not a compound fracture. I'll take my chances as long as you think it's in alignment."

He could see it went against what Gregory thought was best but the thought of having him carve into the leg and put in a rod, or use plates and screws… it made him want to vomit. No, if people in ancient civilizations could recover from fractures using nothing more than splints, a cast and time in bed, he would do the same.

Gregory tried a few more times to persuade him, saying he had portable tools that were powered up before the electricity went out, but eventually he gave up and said he would have to maneuver the leg some more and then he would put it in a long cast.

Landon thanked him while Beth went off to make some tea from herbs that were supposed to assist with pain. The thought of being stranded here for the next two or three months killed him inside but what other option did he have?

Chapter 16

Jake heard the wailing from the truck.

At first it sounded like a cat in pain then the cry became human. He shut off the engine to determine where it was coming from and that's when he was able to pinpoint it. Not wasting a second, he burst out of his vehicle leaving the door wide open as he dashed into the house. "Sara? Sara!" She didn't reply but continued to cry hard. He hurried up the stairs and only came to a halt once he entered the bedroom and saw her sprawled out on top of her mother. It was the most pitiful thing he'd ever seen. There were moments in his life when he was at a loss for words and didn't know what to do; funerals, and someone telling him a loved one had died, this was right up there with that.

He inched forward and placed a hand on her. It was like he'd touched her with a red-hot poker. She wailed louder and gripped her mother as if he was going to pull her away. "Sara," he said multiple times trying to get through to her as anyone might do when they saw someone in pain. Knowing it was better to not interfere, he backed out and went downstairs to wait.

After locking the Scout, he returned to the house and took a seat in a recliner chair looking at the wall. An hour passed in the blink of an eye. His eyes drifted over the family photos on the mantelpiece above the fireplace. One caught his eye, a picture of Sara when she was in her teens. From what he could remember of their school years, sports had been a large part of her life and she'd excelled in track and field. He remembered that's where she'd first caught his eye. Her strong, toned physique, that smile that had by that point in her life broken many a young guy's heart.

Jake got up and browsed. Sara, like many attractive women in high schools, was always out of his reach. It wasn't that he didn't think he could have got a date with her but he'd never been able to summon the nerve to go over and speak with her. She'd surrounded herself with a large group of friends, none of whom were in his circle.

After high school, he went about his life, and she went about hers. Missed opportunities became the norm and eventually he graduated college and assumed she would fly the nest and head off to Bangor or one of the many big cities nearby but she'd stuck around and worked a variety of local jobs. For a while he thought he might stand a chance with her as their paths crossed and he got a sense she was interested.

That all changed with the arrival of Landon.

From there on, it was like he was all she saw.

A shuffle behind him and he cast a glance over his shoulder to see Sara amble into the room, somber with red eyes. He wanted to say something, anything that might offer comfort but he just stood there at a loss for words.

"I took her to see a doctor about her memory. They said she had the signs of early Alzheimer's," Sara muttered looking absently out the window at the snow coming down. "She kept leaving the stove on after cooking dinner. It nearly started a fire. I wanted her at the inn but she wouldn't go. I was supposed to speak with the doctors to see if care might be a solution." Sara wrapped her arms around herself and shook her head as if somehow responsible. She inhaled deeply. "Those windows over there were open. She must have opened and forgot to close them last night. I should have been here. I should have…"

"Sara, you couldn't have known."

"I knew she was struggling."

"And you were seeking help," he said making his way over. He wanted to hold her but knew that could be taken the wrong way.

The sad reality was the elderly would be some of the first to die. Nursing home employees wouldn't show up for work so no one would be there to watch over them and with temperatures dropping, no electricity to keep them warm, and machines not working, it wouldn't take long before people died.

It only brought home the need to prepare. Sure, he

was cutting it short and had only taken care of the vehicle side of things but they still had time.

"What now?" he asked, posing the question to her instead of suggesting they leave her mother. It wasn't like they could bury her in the backyard. The fact was as people died, the dead would stink up the neighborhood if families didn't hurry to bury them. The days of going to a funeral home and making preparations, picking out a casket and compiling a long speech were over. Now it would be a matter of practicality and sanitation to bury the dead as soon as possible. No casket, just a hole in the ground and covering them with soil.

"I don't know," she replied. "I wish Landon was here."

Jake nodded. "Can I make a suggestion?"

She looked at him. He knew he was going out on a limb but he figured it couldn't get any worse than this. "The nearest funeral home is in Bucksport. I can drive you there or…" He swallowed hoping she wouldn't take offense. "We leave your mother here."

"Leave her here?"

And there it was, the frown, the moment she would snap. He had to be tactful.

"If we travel to Bucksport, she'd only be lying there going unattended. At least here it's her home. You can visit until you decide how you want to deal with burial."

The frown faded and inwardly he breathed a sigh of relief. "Yeah, I guess there is no point traveling." She brought a hand to her face and covered her eyes. No more tears fell, though, she just looked as if she was in shock, numb even.

"Do you want to stay or go home?"

"I can't stay here," she said shaking her head. "And anyway I need to get back to Max. Oh Max," she said realizing he would be devastated. "What am I gonna say?"

"Don't say anything," he said.

"What?"

"Look, Sara," Jake took a deep breath. "I'm sorry you've lost your mom, I really am, but there is a time for everything and right now with Landon and Ellie having not returned, the event, and it being Christmas. Word that his grandmother has passed might not be the best thing to share."

"But he'll want to know."

Jake got closer, wanting to reach out and reassure her that everything was going to be okay but he didn't. There were too many variables, and unknowns.

"And he will," he said. "But it's Christmas." He knew what it sounded like before he even said it but after everything that happened so far, he figured the kid could wait a day before being told.

She turned away looking outside where the wind was howling, taunting her almost with the reminder of what it had stolen. "I'm not sure I can do that."

"It's just for one day. Listen, we'll go get some supplies from the grocery store, then I'll drop you home. If you really must tell him, wait until tomorrow. At least that way he can have some semblance of normality before all hell breaks loose." In his mind he was beginning to wonder if Landon and her daughter were even alive. If they weren't, that news alone would destroy them. What harm could waiting one day do?

"No I mean, I don't think I can pretend."

"Of course you can. We all do it every day. We wear masks and hold back saying what we really feel because maybe… maybe we just don't want to destroy what little good we have." Sara looked at him as if trying to decode the double meaning.

Chapter 17

"I'm sorry I can't help you," the nurse said. "The doctor never came in for his shift today."

"But doesn't that strike you as odd?"

The nurse was rifling through folders in a steel cabinet and talking at the same time. "In light of what's happening. No. They're lucky I showed up," the oversized nurse said from behind the counter. Ryerson's Medical Clinic handled a broad range of medical services from pediatrics to geriatrics, gynecology and minor surgery, but anything of significance was referred to Cannon Memorial Hospital which on a good day was thirty minutes away. With roads clogged, dangerous weather and zero power they were looking at an hour or much longer, and that was if they didn't get stopped by someone shooting at them. Okay, the country hadn't exactly gone to hell in a handbasket but it was on its way. Desperation would kick in, and those without would soon prey upon those with too much.

Upon arrival at the clinic, Russ had tried to get information on Dustin. It could be argued that they were grasping at straws in the grand hope that the plane had gone down in their region, he'd survived the crash and managed to make it to the clinic. Russ figured at least if they showed up at the clinic, found out that Dustin wasn't there, they might be open to the idea of leaving. It was either that or return to Cayden and end up being strangled to death. The man had no qualms about killing. They'd already witnessed a few murders that made headlines. He was never linked to them but Russ knew the truth.

"And so you only have the one doctor… what kind of place is this?" he asked because he hadn't grown up in Ryerson nor was he sick often. On the few occasions he'd needed medical attention, like a broken toe or nearly overdosing, he was taken to Cannon Hospital, so this was all new to him.

"Sir, we have a number of physicians but for anyone

requiring minor surgery, that is the responsibility of Dr. Banks. He didn't come in for work. I've already told you that. Now if you don't mind, I'm a little busy."

Russ threw up a hand and turned to the other two who were eavesdropping.

"There you go, boys. Dustin is not here."

"But neither is the doc," Tommy said.

Russ shrugged. "And? Who cares? I say we get out of town now because the odds of us locating that plane are slim to none."

"You heard Cayden," Morgan said.

"Do you really want to trudge through thousands of acres of forest?" He waited for a response but got none. "Exactly. Now even if we did find it, do you honestly think the coke will be in one piece? It's probably scattered from here to Maggie Valley. There's probably cougars and bears getting high right about now. No," he said shaking his head. "I've entertained your ludicrous idea to stop by the clinic but…"

"What if Dustin didn't make it here but the doc went

to him?" Tommy said.

Both of them looked at him with a frown.

"What I mean is, the clinic had multiple physicians, right?" Tommy pointed to a gold plate on the wall that had names of doctors, the floor number they were on and where their office was located. "That nurse only mentioned one doctor not showing up. Think about it. Everyone else is here trying to help except the one man that would be required to perform minor surgery. Doesn't that strike you as a little odd?"

"No. No it doesn't," Russ said. "In fact you don't know he's the only one."

"Well let's find out, shall we?" Tommy turned and headed for the counter where the nurse was still busy rifling through paperwork.

"Tommy. C'mon. This is a waste of time."

"Maybe he's on to something," Morgan said.

"Morgan, what's it smell like up there?"

"Where?"

"Up Cayden's ass because you sure seem to spend a lot

of time there."

Morgan squared up to him but before he could do anything, Tommy came jogging back. "I was right. The other eight physicians are here except him."

"Well that's great news," Russ said. "Let's throw a fucking party and invite him. Oh hold on a minute. That's right. We don't know where he lives and who gives a shit!?"

Tommy shook his finger in front of Russ' nose. "I sometimes wonder about your mental state. It's not rocket science," he said crossing the lobby. They followed him to two dilapidated phones. Why they still existed was beyond him. They were the last of a dying era. Tommy opened a phone book beneath one and thumbed through it. He flipped a few thin pages and then ran his finger down, mumbling under his breath.

Morgan wasn't done with Russ. He jabbed his arm with a fist. "What were you saying about Cayden?"

Before Russ could say anything, Tommy turned and held up the book. "See." He was pointing to the name

Gregory Banks. "Ryerson might be a small, shitty, insignificant town to you but it means finding people isn't hard." Right beside his name was an address. Tommy ripped the page out and made a beeline for the exit. Morgan followed, glaring at him.

Russ remained there contemplating leaving by himself. But where would he go? "Damn it," he said before taking off after them.

Chapter 18

Exhausted from the hike home, Gregory tossed his keys on the kitchen counter and kicked his boots off. His dark Siamese cat slalomed around his legs as he called out to his wife. "Nancy. I'm home." Years in medicine as an affluent doctor had paid off allowing him to purchase a home nestled away in the forest. It had also given him the choice of working for the hospital or a slow-paced clinic. After reaching the age of fifty he opted for the latter.

He'd been devastated when he'd heard the news of Sierra Sullivan's passing. A close friend and colleague, she had bonded with him over their love of medicine and if he'd been twenty years younger, he probably would have dated her.

That's why when Beth showed up on his doorstep he couldn't refuse to help. He was meant to go into the clinic that morning and under any other circumstances he would have been there but with the weather the way it was and her showing up, he figured they could manage for one day.

"Nancy. You there, hon?" he said scooping up unopened mail and thumbing it open as he walked into the living room. He lifted his eyes to find her sitting on a sofa, a rag in her mouth, her wrists and feet bound and two men either side of her; one with a gun stuck into her rib cage. "Who the...?"

The fist blindsided him from the right, knocking him to the ground.

A second of seeing stars and a meaty paw grabbed him and dragged him to his feet, tossing him into his recliner chair. "Take a seat, doctor." A third man came into view. He was brash, and had wild hair that looked as if it hadn't been washed in weeks.

"You want money. I can give it to you. Just don't hurt her."

The man stood a few feet in front of him. "Money isn't much use to us now."

"Then food. Take whatever you want."

"Oh we plan on doing that but first things first." He crossed the room and opened a cabinet. Took out a bottle of expensive scotch and twisted the cap off. He poured out two fingers and downed it before tossing the bottle to the Chinese-looking fella on the couch. "Nancy said you were in the mountains today. Is that right?"

"What's that to you?"

"Answer the question."

When he hesitated, the large muscular one squeezed Nancy's knee hard making her squeal.

"Yes. Yes. Okay. I was there. Leave her alone."

"Very good, Gregory. Now for ten points can you tell me why? You see, Nancy here didn't know; you seemed to have glossed over that part unless of course she was telling a lie. Were you, Nancy?" The guy shifted his weight from one foot to the next.

"I was doing a favor for a friend of mine," Gregory said.

"Ooh, getting warmer but I'm gonna need a few more details."

Gregory sighed. "There was a patient. What do you want to know?"

"That patient wouldn't go by the name Dustin, would he?"

"No, that was the pilot. He didn't survive."

"Ah, now we are getting somewhere." He walked behind Gregory and placed his hands on his shoulders and began squeezing them like he was attempting to give him a massage. "Then who the hell was on that plane? You see, because Dustin flies alone."

He shook his head. "I don't know what you're talking about."

The man patted him and walked around to look him in the eye.

"Come on, keep up, Gregory. Who was the patient?"

"Someone traveling to Maine."

"Anyone else?"

"No."

"And the problem?"

"Broken legs."

The man sucked in air. "Oooooh, that's gotta hurt."

He cocked his head to one side and stared at Gregory as if contemplating. Gregory looked over at Nancy and tried to reassure her that everything would be okay.

"So who told you about this patient?"

"A friend."

"Male. Female? Young, old? What are we talking about here?"

"Look, is there something you want? Because you're scaring my wife."

He laughed. "Oh we are? You scared, Nancy?" he asked as if expecting her to tell him the truth. She nodded her head.

"At least remove the gag in her mouth."

"Answer the question."

"Her name's Beth Sullivan, okay? She's seventeen. A friend of the family."

That must have caught his attention as he saw the way the man's eyes lit up. In a small town, reputations traveled fast and anyone who was anyone in the town knew her father. "Rhett and Sierra's kid?"

"Yes. You know them?" Gregory's eyes widened wondering if they were friends.

The man dodged the question. "Look. Did this patient tell you where the plane went down?"

"No. I was there to help, then I left."

The man walked over to the table and scooped up an apple out of a fruit bowl and took a huge bite. He munched it in a sloppy fashion "Okay. So where is this patient?"

A knot formed in Gregory's stomach. Why did they want to know? He was hesitant to say anything out of fear for Beth's safety. If men would barge into his house and do this, what would they do to her?

"Does it really matter?"

The man paused in mid-bite. He turned to his two pals and laughed. "He wants to know if it matters." He looked back at him. "Gregory, you're a doctor, would you open up someone if it didn't matter?" He waited for a response but he didn't give him one. "Why the hell would we be in your home if it didn't matter?" His voice got louder. He tossed the apple at the wall and it exploded, chunks raining down. "Where is this patient staying!?" he bellowed, leaning forward and getting in Gregory's face. "Or would you like us to ask Nancy?"

"She doesn't know."

"Exactly. But I'm sure she can convince you."

His face went blank. When he didn't reply immediately the man pulled a handgun from the back of his waistband, marched over to Nancy and pointed at her head. From behind the rag she screamed. Gregory went to get up but was quickly thrust back into his seat by one of his pals. "An address, Gregory!" he yelled. "Or I'm gonna repaint this room with you beloved wife's brain matter."

"I can't give you an exact location because I don't know it. But I can draw you a map."

The man uncocked his revolver. "Perfect. Tommy, get this man some paper and a pen."

The Chinese fella got up and went over to where the phone was and snatched up a pad of paper and a pen. He handed it to Gregory and they stood over him while he sketched out the directions from his place to the turn-off road. "It's not easy to find. She guided me to it in a damn snowstorm. This is the best I can offer," he said handing the pad back. He glanced at Nancy and gave a strained smile.

"Well, I would thank you, Gregory, but now I'm starting to wonder, can I really be sure unless I take you with me?"

"I just got back. I don't remember."

"I think you do. You made it back on your own which tells me you didn't have any difficulty finding the way."

"It's a lot different coming down a mountain in the day than at night."

"Well I guess we'll just have to see. In the meantime, one of us will stay with Nancy until we confirm."

"No, I can't go with you."

"Oh but you can," he said. He pointed to the one called Tommy. "Get him up."

Gregory knew that this wouldn't end well. Leaving

Nancy alone with one of those animals. He didn't want to imagine what could happen. He eyed the gun in the front of Tommy's jeans as he walked over. If he could just... Tommy reached out to grab him and in that moment he went for it. As Tommy pulled him up, he lunged forward, going for the gun. He fell on top of Tommy and felt the brunt force of someone striking him on the head while Nancy screamed.

Before they pulled him off, he managed to get the gun out of the waistband but Tommy had hold of it. They rolled and then it erupted. The sound echoed loudly and he felt fire in his gut. It was undeniable. Agonizing pain but with shock his scream caught in his throat. Tommy rolled him off and stood over him as he bled out on the ground. He heard Nancy screaming and watched the world around him fade to black.

Chapter 19

"How did your mother die?" He cut her off as she spoon-fed him soup and was telling him how she'd carved the bowl by hand. She couldn't believe he'd asked the question. Was he delirious from the medication? Who asked how someone died? Wasn't that a taboo area that anyone with a lick of common sense stayed clear of? It was something she wouldn't even discuss with her father let alone a complete stranger.

Beth stopped feeding him and got up and walked away.

"I'm sorry. I…" he said.

With her back turned to him she dropped the bowl into a sink of murky water and looked at her reflection. Beth gripped the counter tightly trying to hold in the fresh grief that had overlapped the past. She still hadn't told him that her father was dead, maybe because she didn't believe it herself. Beth looked at her father's jacket hung on the back of the door. She was expecting him to walk in any minute. She could hear his voice as clear as day. It was quickly replaced by Landon's. "Beth."

Beth didn't look at him but snatched up her jacket and bow, whistled to Grizzly and headed out letting him feel the stupidity of his question. Outside with the door closed, she sucked air in fast. *Stop crying. Stop crying.* Her father's words rang in her ears, the memory of the day came back to sting her heart. *You need to be strong now.*

How could she be when he wasn't here to guide her, care for her or show her the way forward? The bleakness of her own situation far outweighed the one facing the town. Living without electricity had been a way of life for so long that it didn't bother her to learn that an EMP had occurred. It was the loss of parents that pained her. No one would get to see her graduate. No one would be there to walk her down the aisle. But worst of all, no one would be there for her to show the same kindness in their old age as they had with her while she was young. It wasn't meant to be like this.

Beth and Grizzly trudged through the snow making their way back to the wreckage. She'd promised to see if she could find a brown satchel he'd been carrying. He wouldn't go into why he needed it, only that it was important. In addition, she'd already promised to see what had become of his daughter even though she knew Ellie was dead. Grizzly looked like he was bouncing on a trampoline as he led the way. The plane or what was left of it was located a few miles southeast of the cabin. The sky was bright, the snow almost blinding as the last of the sun dipped behind the surrounding pines. It had been a miserable walk with gusts of wind churning up the powdery snow. Whatever warmth she felt before leaving the cabin was now gone. Her jeans were once again soaked.

If it wasn't for the trees that had been torn asunder, she was certain that finding the plane would have been near impossible. The forest was so dense and thick it was easy for the trees to swallow a small charter plane.

Her eyes spotted it covered in snow, the inner guts still

exposed but now filled with a slope of snow. Great, she muttered to herself. Digging through snow when she was already chilled to the bone was not ideal but a promise was a promise.

Beth created a path in the snow using her machete like a paddle to push snow behind her. She crawled on her hands and knees until she was inside the plane and near the seat Landon had been in. He said the satchel had been shoved under the seat. Using her hands she scooped out snow until her fingers caught on leather. Finally. She tugged it until it came loose and she fell back against the remains of the pilot. Startled, Beth placed a hand over her heart and took a second to catch her breath. A wintry gust of air blew in and she lowered her face to avoid its bite.

It was then she saw it.

The handle of a bag sticking out of snow. Curious, and wondering if it might have belonged to Landon, she crawled forward and began raking at the snow to reveal the rest. It was a large green duffel bag. Once she managed to pry it loose, Beth sat back on her knees and unzipped it. Upon opening it her jaw went slack. She fished in and retrieved a brick of white wrapped in cellophane and tape. She used the tip of her machete to stab it and investigate further. Beth already had an idea of what it was but she wanted to be sure. She dipped a finger in and smelled it. The same familiar sweet, pungent, almost flower-ish smell. It was damp and sticky powder. Beth dabbed a finger of it onto the tip of her tongue to taste it, then grimaced at how bitter it was.

A surge of anger rose. A flood of memories.

She gritted her teeth as she shoved it back into the bag and zipped it up. She slung the bag over her shoulder, and carried the satchel. She was determined to have words with Landon once she got back. She had a good mind to go back immediately but first the girl, if only for her sake.

Beth scanned the hilly terrain, and the path of destruction that had cut through the forest. How far had it traveled, clipping the trees before the fuselage broke apart and the tail disappeared? The back end could be anywhere. "C'mon boy," she said pointing west and squinting. So much snow had already fallen, at least two feet and it was still coming down, not as hard but it was enough to hide a body. Along the way pieces of steel stuck out from the snow. She couldn't begin to imagine what it must have been like to die that way. Had it been fast? Would his daughter have passed out or felt everything? Did she die instantly or suffer for a while until taking her last breath?

Lost in thought she almost overlooked it. It was Grizzly's bark that alerted her, then him returning with something in his mouth. "What you got there, boy?" She crouched and took out a piece of what looked like a skirt. She gazed around. A mound of snow farther down, just off the path where the plane had cut into the forest, appeared out of place.

It was only when Beth made her way over and reached out to touch the snow that she realized what it was. A large chunk slid off and she turned her head and closed her eyes. It was a seat upside down, sticking out of the snow. Beth pulled the machete from a sheath around her back and used it to dig into the snow. As ice had fallen with the snow the previous evening, some areas were harder than others. As she shoveled, a gust of snow erased her hard work. The wind howled in her ears as she continued digging until she saw a hand. It wasn't much bigger than her own.

She wanted to stop right then and walk away but Ellie deserved better.

Grizzly got involved pawing at the snow, hurling it back beneath his legs while she dug deep to release the seat. The more she saw of the young girl, the harder it was. Beads of sweat formed on her brow as she sat back on her knees to catch a breath.

Death was hard to see.

She remembered the first time she saw her mother.

She recalled stepping into the building and making her way up to the casket. It was the strangest thing ever. Her mother looked just as beautiful as she did in life. But this, this body before her now was awful. Though the cold had preserved the body, some small animals had managed to burrow their way in and chew flesh from the bone.

Another gust of wind blew in her face. "I'll get you out," she said as if Ellie could hear her. Beth cut the seat belt that still held the girl. Her body was frozen into a position of horror. Her face agape, terrorized by her final seconds.

Beth continued digging until she was able to drag the body a short distance. She shrugged off her backpack and pulled out a large black plastic bag and covered her frozen body as best as she could before beginning to drag her back up the slope. Of course she wouldn't let Landon see her like this. No one deserved to see their loved one in this horrific state. Once her body had thawed, she would remove the clothes and dress her in something of her own, cover her face in makeup and then place her in one of the sheds before having a funeral. It felt morbid, nothing like dragging an animal carcass home. Beth kept stopping every few minutes and asking Ellie to forgive her.

What was she like? she wondered. What had been her

dreams?

Her own loss soon subsided at the thought of what Landon would never get to do. He would never walk her down the aisle, hold her children or see what she would make of her life. In some ways they were the same, and yet so different.

As she made her way up, she heard the crack of a gun, and two more rounds.

Was it hunters?

She was tempted to go and see but she didn't want to leave the body out. Animals were prone to dragging away meat. Beth pressed on, thinking of what the future would hold now that both of them had lost loved ones.

Chapter 20

They were too late.

Forty-eight hours, that's all it had taken to wipe out the store. It reminded her of the aftermath of Black Friday at the Walmart Supercenter. Bare shelves everywhere including behind the counter. It wasn't looters, just straight up cash purchases from locals. They were all too familiar with how things worked in a power outage. Survival depended on it. She recalled seeing two people almost end up in a fight over a case of water last year. It was nuts. They could have traveled half an hour to Hannaford Supermarket in Bucksport or fifty minutes to the Walmart near Ellsworth but that would have meant going out of their way, and why do that when they could fight over meager pickings?

To be fair at least their vehicles were working last year.

This was completely different.

Sara sighed, could this day get any worse? She stood

there wide-eyed in T & C Grocery looking at what remained. There were no large chain grocery stores in Castine, Maine, nor in Penobscot nearby. Castine only offered one choice, a tiny mom-and-pop store that provided a small selection of foods including breads, meats, cheeses, pizzas, and sandwiches, plus cigarettes, liquor and so on. After spending most of his life in Florida, Landon would joke that it reminded him more of a convenience store than a grocery, and he wasn't that far wrong.

Still, it was local and the owners were friendly.

However, that was of no use to her now.

"There is a pack of cheese Doritos. You want those?" Jake laughed finding humor in the moment. "I told you we should have stopped at the Walmart on the way back."

He'd wanted to get in line with a massive crowd of five hundred people, and most of those were outside, but she wanted to get back to her son. And anyway, she figured by the time they made it into Walmart, the shelves would have probably been stripped. Sara believed that T & C would have enough. It didn't.

"Sorry, Sara," Meg Cullen said. "There was a surge of people earlier today. I certainly made my money. Gotta love these storms."

Meg was a feisty woman with pink spiky hair who posted videos online of people attempting to steal items from her store. According to her she actually made some good money from it, and had gained a lot of subscribers.

"It's not just a storm," Sara said before Jake put a hand up to caution her. She waved him off. If there was one thing that mattered to her it was this small town and if he was right, and this was a countrywide disaster, she felt it behooved her to give others the heads-up. She wouldn't have wanted to be left in the dark.

"What? Of course it is."

"Meg, you tried starting your car?"

"No, I figured it was too cold."

"Well, you'll see," she said heading for the doorway.

"Hey uh, Sara." Meg raised a finger. "I do have a few items in the back you might be interested in but the price tag will be a lot higher."

"How much higher? You already charge an arm and a leg."

She grinned. "Gotta make a living."

There was no one else in the store, otherwise she figured Meg wouldn't have said anything.

Sara forced a smile. "What have you got?"

"That depends, you got the green?"

Sara held up a wad.

Excited by the opportunity to make more cash, she hurried to the front door and locked it before turning the open sign to closed. "Can't be too careful. Had a few people in here earlier on that were irate."

She shoved a large set of jangling keys into her jeans before eyeing Jake as she led them out back. In the rear were a few boxes of canned goods, mostly vegetables, tuna and some pasta. "It's not much but it's yours for the right price."

"What are we talking?"

"Twenty bucks a can."

"Are you serious?"

"The last can of beans I sold went for fifteen. Supply and demand, baby, supply and demand."

She blew out her cheeks and looked at Jake and he nodded. Not one to be ripped off, he tried to get her to reduce the price but she wouldn't budge so Sara thumbed off the cash and paid for twenty cans, five bags of pasta and a bottle of red wine as she planned on getting drunk, and that was something she rarely did. "Nice doing business with you," Meg said placing the cash into a safety box that she secured with a key on a chain before placing that chain over her neck. They watched it drop into her breasts.

Jake gave Sara a hand carrying out the box.

"What a rip-off."

"Ah the cash won't be much use to her."

As they stepped outside, two guys and a girl in their early twenties were attempting to break into the Scout. "Hey!" Jake yelled, hurrying over. They dropped a Slim Jim lock pick. The long strip of metal clattered on the ground. Jake placed the box on the ground and took off after them leaving Sara to look at the damage. It was minimal. A few scrapes. Fortunately they hadn't managed to unlock it. Jake returned a few minutes later, cursing under his breath. "They steal anything?'

"They never got in."

"Good." He unlocked the door and threw the box in the rear. "I'll have to hide this. With few vehicles on the road, people will want to get their hands on it."

He fired up the engine and they drove off heading for the Manor.

"I still don't get it. Why is this working?"

"Like I told you. Most of the vehicles today rely on electronics. This baby doesn't. In fact those two vehicles we saw on the way out to Trenton were similar to this. They were probably diesel, had a large fuel tank, good cargo space, and towing and off-road capability." He asked her to get a pack of cigarettes out of the glove compartment. She reached down and a large box dropped out. She glanced at him. "What? I was saving them for a rainy day," he said with a smile. She'd never smoked a day in her life. The smell was foul. "Anyway, parts are a little easier to find for these than some souped-up, expensive modern vehicle. Then of course, the most important thing — this baby doesn't rely on microelectronics, computers or chips. I remember the client, the one that recommended I get one, gave me a whole list of things to avoid when it came to searching for a vehicle. He also said, make sure it doesn't stand out. Hence the reason this sucker has a camouflage paint job. It also has a conductive metal body enclosing the engine and passenger compartment. Well, I slightly customized it but for the most part it's just the way it was when I got it from the auction."

He rattled on spouting all manner of stuff that went over her head. In all honesty her mind was elsewhere — with Landon and Ellie. Where were they?

As they got closer to the Manor, Jake kept sweeping the mirrors.

Sara glanced behind her shoulder but didn't see

anything.

"You okay?" she asked.

"Yeah, I swore I saw something. Nah, was probably nothing."

He drove up the long driveway, the tires crunching over snow as a flurry washed across the windshield. "Looks like the weather is getting worse. Lucky you got this," he said jerking his head towards the food.

"Listen, Jake, I really appreciate all you've done. You didn't have to go out of your way."

"No. I know. Glad to help."

Sara hopped out and he gave her a hand taking the box into the kitchen.

"Do you want to stay for supper? With it being Christmas and all."

"I appreciate the offer but I should be getting back."

"You live alone, Jake," she said.

"Thanks for reminding me," he said, his lip curling into a smile

"Oh. I didn't mean it like that. I... Uh, sorry." She

tucked her hands into the front of her jeans and bit down on the lower portion of her lip.

He shrugged. "It's fine."

"Jake. I've gotta ask. Why aren't you with someone? I always figured by now you would be…"

"Happily married?"

She nodded.

"Are you?" he asked, turning the question back on her.

She didn't reply immediately because he caught her off guard. "Ah, I shouldn't have asked. Forget it. Well I should get back to it. If you change your mind, we'll probably eat around six." He nodded, said he would consider it and made his way out. Sara went over to the window and glanced out, watching him get back into the vehicle. She would have been lying to say she wasn't attracted to him. He had this boyish charm that appealed to her. Then again, Landon had his strong points. She was happy. Wasn't she? She shook the doubt from her mind and went to stock the cupboard.

"Max. I could use a hand."

Unlike days gone by, when she usually had to go up and pull his earbuds out, he came bounding down the stairs. "You're back. I didn't hear you return?"

"Well maybe if you take those earbuds out once in a while you wouldn't have ear damage," she said joking with him. He looked around.

"Jake gone home?"

"Yeah. But he might be joining us for dinner."

"What about Dad, Ellie? Any sign of them at the airport?"

She reached into the box and pulled out a can and sighed, shaking her head. Max looked as concerned as she was. "I'm sure they're fine. You know your father. He's probably enjoying the warmth of Alabama right about now."

"How would he?" Max said. "The country has no power."

"How did you find out?"

"I'm not deaf," he said.

"You were listening to our conversation?"

"Not exactly… your voice travels…" He pointed to the large vents. She tipped her head back and smiled as she returned to the pantry and added a few more cans.

Max looked in the box. "Is that it?"

She sighed. "I'm afraid so. And if Jake is right it might be the last of it for a while."

"The last of it?" He frowned.

Over the next twenty minutes she outlined what Jake had shared with her and the chance of things getting worse as people started to realize the gravity of the situation. Under normal conditions, generally people remained calm when there was a power outage, that's because emergency services were still operational, water flowed, communication often still worked and vehicles could be relied upon, but now that had all been stripped away. Remembering what Jake said, Sara picked up the landline and listened for a dial tone. It was still there but for how long? And what was the point of a few old landlines working if most phones in homes and businesses were no longer operational?

"Do we even have a turkey?"

She brought a hand up to her head and frowned. "Shoot, the turkey. I put it out to thaw but didn't put it on to cook." Max groaned then fished into the box. "Well, I guess it's pasta tonight then. That will be a first," he said.

They both laughed as she scooped up the wine and put an arm around him. He was a good kid, certainly more understanding than Landon was at times.

"Oh, I forgot to tell you. Hank came by while you were out. I told him you'd gone with Jake to the airport."

"What did he want?"

Max shrugged. "No clue. He said he would swing by later." She knew that asking him for a ride was a dumb idea. He was the kind of man that if you gave him an inch, he would take a mile. He was known to cheat on his wife. Sara had avoided his advances numerous times, and she was still living down the embarrassment of when Landon knocked Hank on his ass. Sure, he'd tried to come on to her but that was when he was drunk.

Generally when he wasn't drinking, he was cordial and polite but maybe that was because others were around.

The generator could be heard churning away.

"I hope you haven't had that on all the time I've been out?" she said.

"It's freezing."

"I know but we need it for tonight and there's not a lot of gasoline left. Once that runs out—"

"Why didn't you buy a solar one?" Max asked.

"Because it cost too much. We were lucky to get that at the price we did."

After finishing unpacking, she began preparing for a light supper; tuna and pasta with onions. Something simple and quick. It wasn't ideal but maybe with a glass of wine she could pretend it was a delicious, mouthwatering turkey.

As she was reading the side of the box the generator shut off.

"Max? Can you get that?"

He didn't respond. Sara groaned and slipped back into

her jacket and boots and waded out into knee-deep snow. It was still coming down heavy and if it kept going, at this rate they would be snowed in. She rubbed her hands together, her breath releasing in puffs of smoke before her as she made her way to the generator. She figured because Max had been using it while they were out that it needed topping up. She unscrewed the top and looked inside. It wasn't full but it wasn't empty. What the hell? She stared at the generator and turned it back on again. Once it fired up, she pulled a face and headed back inside not giving it another thought. Maybe the cold had shut it off. No, that was impossible.

Two minutes, that's all it took and it shut off again.

"Oh you have got to be shitting me," she said, then apologized to the Lord above. She wasn't a religious person but having grown up with a mother who never missed a Sunday, she had gained a conscience, a kind of moral meter that attempted to keep her in check. Trudging back out to the generator, this time she noticed something different. There were footsteps leading up to and away from the generator, none of which originated from the house. How hadn't she seen that before?

A shot of fear went through her.

Sara scanned the property, backing up slowly while glancing over her shoulder.

Who was out there? Hidden by the storm? And why were they shutting off the generator? One thought went through her mind — get Landon's rifle.

Chapter 21

The cougar attacked and nearly got the drop on Cayden. Russ had reacted fast, firing two rounds which echoed loudly. One struck the snarling beast in its hindquarter. It scampered away leaving a trail of blood behind and Cayden in a state of shock. Russ extended a hand to help him up, but instead of accepting it, he waved him off.

Embarrassed, he got up and brushed off snow. "I'm fine. Let's just find that coke and get off this damn mountain," he bellowed.

Morgan grinned and shook his head as he trudged ahead leading the group of four using the vague scribblings of the doctor.

Cayden and Morgan walked ahead of them, discussing business while Russ hung back with Tommy. "You don't think he'll say anything, do you?" Russ asked Tommy.

"Morgan? No. He's a good man. A few screws loose

but he's got your back."

"He better or he might find something buried in his back," Russ said as he lifted his boots out of the deep snow. It felt like they were wading through quicksand.

"I really wish you hadn't shot him," Russ said referring to the doctor.

"I had no choice, he was all over me. It was either him or me. For a second I thought I'd taken the bullet."

"And the wife?"

"She was a witness. We couldn't leave her there."

Russ shook his head. Illegal activities were one thing, killing wasn't something he was onboard with. Morgan had no qualms about it, especially if it meant impressing Cayden but Tommy, he thought he was better than that.

"I've become something I never wanted," Russ said.

Tommy scratched the side of his face. "It was inevitable, Russ. What did you think you'd be doing if you managed to scrape some off the top?"

Russ flashed him a glare and put a finger to his lips. "Keep it down," he said.

"Sorry."

"I got into this to make money not to murder people."

"It kind of comes with the territory, don't you think?"

"No. We have choices," Russ said. "Morgan didn't need to kill those cops."

Tommy nodded. "Yeah, maybe," he muttered.

Although snow was still falling and had covered Dr. Banks' tracks, and the map was vague, it was enough to point them in the right direction. They saw the gouge in the forest long before the plane or what was left of it. Morgan hollered, "I got something."

He charged ahead and ran out into a clearing.

When the rest of them caught up, Cayden looked off to the east and west. "Which way?" Tommy asked.

Morgan pointed to the treetops. "See how much has been clipped to the west versus the east? It's that way," he said heading to the east. The mountainside was covered in snow and at times was slippery, especially where there were rocks jutting out. It was clear to see that very few people came up this high, and yet someone had been here.

"I've got fresh tracks!" Morgan said, dropping to a crouch and putting a hand into a footprint, then looking up ahead at the row of tracks. "Looks like the same person went both ways."

"Searching?" Tommy asked.

"Or carrying away something," Cayden said, motioning to what appeared to be a large gouge in the snow as if someone was dragging a sleigh.

This was not going to end well, Russ thought. He had got used to gauging Cayden's mood swings after having him tag along on a couple of deals. In every instance when he'd gone with them it ended with him going berserk on one of the men. His lack of trust was evident. Now it seemed that they were one step away from seeing another outburst.

Continuing on, it didn't take long to find the plane buried with tracks leading in and out. Cayden was the first inside, scrambling around with a hand-cranked flashlight on. "There's Dustin but where's my coke?" He turned and bellowed, "C'mon, help me find it." Over the next hour they searched high and low for the bag but came up empty-handed. Cayden paced, fury building in his features.

"It could have been in the tail."

"Have you ever known Dustin to leave it in the tail? No. It's always behind that seat," Cayden said pointing. "There's only one other person that's been near this plane." He stared down at the small boot prints and began to follow them. Cayden cradled his AR-15 and forged ahead.

Chapter 22

It took only a few breathless seconds for Sara to realize someone was playing games. She'd turned to dash back into the house when her world was rocked. The collision was so hard and unexpected she thought her nose broke from the impact. Looming over her, blocking the last rays of sunlight, a figure extended a hand, apologizing profusely.

"Whoa, I'm so sorry. I thought you heard me."

"Hank? Hank!" she bellowed, glaring at him as he hauled her up. Blood gushed down from her nose, droplets hitting the snow. She groaned and placed a hand to her head. She felt a little woozy. Sara staggered to the side, and he caught her with a chuckle.

"Come on, let's get you inside and get that cleaned up." He continued to apologize as he led her through the mud room into the kitchen where Max was devouring a sandwich and packet of chips, completely unaware of what had just transpired. He glanced up and his eyes widened.

"It's okay. Just a little accident," Hank said, bringing her over to a seat where he got her to sit. "Just keep your head back."

"An accident? An accident is when I stub my foot, or spill a drink," Sara said. "What the hell are you doing creeping up on people?" The sink was full of water that she'd filled to the brim. Hank took out a bowl and scooped up some and then dipped a rag in it and brought it over to her face to wash away the crimson stain.

"I wasn't creeping. Like I said, I thought you heard me." He lifted his hands and grimaced, realizing he'd made a mistake.

Sara dabbed at her nose, then washed the rag in the bowl of water. "So was that you who turned off the generator?"

"Yes."

"Why?"

He groaned. "I was about to refill it with fuel," he said.

He quickly headed out of the house and returned a moment later with a red gasoline canister that he held up as evidence. "I swung by earlier and spoke to Max, I asked him if there was anything you needed. He said you were a little low on gasoline. I figured I'd bring over some of the extra that we have. When I arrived, I turned off the generator, then walked back to my truck to collect the canister and it came on again. I thought the damn thing was faulty."

"So did I!" she bellowed before getting up and going over to the sink. "Maybe next time before you decide to show up unannounced, call me."

"A little hard when you don't pick up."

"What are you talking about? The landline is…" She picked it up and now there was no dial tone. "That's odd, it was working only a short time ago. Did you say yours was working?"

"It was before I left home. I mean, the landline." He walked over and checked hers. Sure enough there was no dial tone. "Huh, strange."

Sara waved him off, too tired to get into it. Jake had warned her that it would eventually stop, she just figured it would last at least a week. "Listen, thanks for bringing by gasoline but I can't pay you for it. I already spent the cash I had on groceries."

"You don't need to pay me. It's a gift."

"Come on, Hank. There's always strings attached with you."

He laughed. "Can't a neighbor just do something nice for once?"

She narrowed her gaze but decided not to say what was on her mind. Hank rarely went out of his way to do anything for anyone in the town unless it affected his bottom line or gave him some form of sexual gratification. Hank looked around the kitchen. "So you managed to wrangle some food from Meg's place?"

"What little she had," Sara said before taking a seat because she felt lightheaded. She kept the cloth near her face. She hadn't had a nosebleed since she was nine and that had happened at Christmas. She'd come barreling down the stairs behind her cousin who was visiting and went smack bang into the back of her. She was beginning to wonder if her Christmases were cursed.

Hank sniffed the air. "I would have thought you'd have a turkey cooking by now, with the generator and the time and…" Oh he knew how to play the game. "You know what, Rita has a beautiful one cooking right now. More than enough for us. Why don't you two come on back? Heck, you could stay the night. I mean, Landon hasn't returned yet, has he?"

He knew full well he hadn't.

"Listen, I appreciate the offer but we're just—"

"I would love that," Max said. "We were only gonna have pasta and tuna."

Hank grimaced. "Pasta and tuna on Christmas Day? Oh there has to be some law against that," he said, a smile forming. His eyes bounced between them. "Well then it's done. You'll both come back with me."

He was so damn pushy. This was exactly why Landon punched him. He came across as friendly but everything he did was manipulative. He reminded her of a sleazy Hollywood executive that wined and dined actresses just so he could corner them later in a hotel room under the pretense of offering them a role.

"Hank. It's not a good time," she said raising a hand.

"Of course it is. It's Christmas. And besides, after what we've been through over the past few days, I think celebrating with a drink, and having a laugh over a nice meal is exactly what we all need."

With you? No thanks, she thought.

"Nope. I insist. Grab your stuff and I'll run you over. Rita will be over the moon."

Hardly. Was that poor woman blind? Sara could already see how the night would play out. Hank would get her liquored up and then when Rita stepped out and Max was busy with some gift, he'd make his move.

Max dashed out of the room and up the stairs as quick as a flash. Sara used the opportunity to get out of the situation before Max returned. "Look, I really would love to spend Christmas with you both but…" She didn't need to pretend, the pain was still fresh. "My mother is dead."

It was the quickest way to put the brakes on.

"What?" he asked.

She quickly explained and told him not to say anything to Max. As hard-headed as Hank could be, even he knew it was best to back off. "I'm sorry to hear that, Sara. Um. Look, if you change your mind. You know where we are."

"Thank you," she said, walking over to the door to lead him out.

Hank stopped and looked at her for a second as if he was about to say something then he opted to just continue on out. As Hank fired up his vehicle and pulled out, Max came dashing down the stairs, wide-eyed and ready to leave. "Where's Hank?"

"He's heading home. We're not going."

"But I thought—"

"Something came up. He had to leave."

"Or you drove him away."

"No. I…"

"It's meant to be Christmas. It's freezing in this house and he…"

"I know what he offered, Max," she said before sighing. "It's just not a good time."

"When is it ever?" he said storming out of the room.

"Max, c'mon. Max!"

He didn't answer.

Now she felt bad. Okay, Hank had gone about it the wrong way but he was trying to do something nice. They could have gone over and enjoyed a meal, but she wanted to be here when Landon returned, and of course she'd already invited Jake to join them for supper. Sara went over to the bottle of wine and poured another glass. This was going to be a long Christmas.

Chapter 23

The door of the cabin burst open. Grizzly bounded in shaking off a coat of snow. Beth followed, shrugging off a large duffel bag and sliding it across the floor towards him. "You want to tell me about this?" she said before dropping his satchel on a chair nearby. He stared at it for a second and then shook his head.

"What is it?"

She raised a hand. "You tell me."

"Beth, you've lost me," he said grimacing and motioning for his satchel. She glanced at it and then looked back at him. "My bag. Can you…?"

"Once you answer the question," she said.

He frowned, confused. "It's not mine. I've never seen it before."

"Bullshit!" she yelled.

His eyes got big. "I've never seen it," he repeated.

"Never seen it? Really. Because it was under the seat

across from where you sat on the plane." Nothing was registering so she continued. "Maybe this will refresh your memory." She got up and unzipped the bag and then tossed one of the bricks over. Landon caught it, his eyes darting from the one brick to the bag.

"This was on the plane?"

She shook her head. "Don't act surprised. You know it was."

"Beth. I didn't know about this. I mean…" he trailed off and looked as if he knew something but wasn't letting on.

"You were about to say?"

He looked at a loss for words. "The pilot said he did drop-offs. This must have been what he was referring to." He groaned. "Ugh. It makes sense."

She inhaled deeply and leaned forward with her arms folded. "So I'm supposed to believe you knew nothing about that?"

"Yes. Hell, I didn't even know the pilot. My boss arranged the ride. He…" Again he stopped, this time bringing a hand up to his mouth.

"You were about to say?"

"My boss had a drug habit. I…"

"What are you not telling me?"

He puffed out his cheeks and screwed his eyes shut. "I can't believe it. That bastard! I knew I should have parted ways with him."

"What are you talking about?"

"It doesn't matter. What matters is I knew nothing about that."

She went over and turned the duffel bag over letting every brick bounce against the hardwood floor of the cabin. "You got on a plane with your daughter and you didn't know about this?"

"That's what I just said," he shot back looking a little annoyed.

She gritted her teeth and shook her head then turned and headed for the door.

"Beth. Beth! Even if I knew, why does it matter to you?"

She spun around, her face a picture of anger. "You asked me how my mother died." She jabbed her finger at the bag. "That's how!"

Beth flung the door open.

"Where are you going?"

The door slammed shut leaving him alone with her dog. She heard Grizzly scratching at the door and whining. It was rare for him to see her angry but in that moment she was furious. She didn't know what to believe. Was it likely that someone who was involved in drug running would admit to it? Was it possible he'd got on the flight and not been told about the bag?

Angry and unsure of what to say, she looked over at Ellie's body and decided to take her into the shed nearby and lift the body onto a large wooden workbench. It wasn't ideal but it was out of the gale and it would give her a chance to ask Landon if he wanted to see her before she was buried. Morbid? Yes. But not any more than if he'd witnessed her body out there in the piles of snow.

Chapter 24

Christmas at the Grays' home that year was depressing. From the kitchen, Sara glanced into the living room at the untouched Christmas presents under the tree. Max refused to open his until Ellie returned. There had been no word from Landon besides that single voice message. And with her mom gone, and no shoulder to cry on, it only made it that much harder. Sara was at her wits' end. She didn't think anything could be worse than having the country on the brink of disaster. But this tragedy had overshadowed it all. She felt powerless and out of control.

The only thing she was grateful for was that damn generator — and that wouldn't last long, of that she was sure but for now it would provide enough power to switch on multiple appliances. She stirred a pot of pasta and called up to Max to come down as she'd be serving soon. Sara had held off preparing the food, thinking Jake would show but he didn't. It was now closing in on seven and was dark outside. Sara drained off the hot water. Steam billowed up around her face before she emptied the contents into a bowl and added tuna. Outside the motion sensor must have detected an animal as it flashed on lighting up the grounds that led down to Battle Avenue. Sara glanced out the window. It wasn't uncommon to have a rabbit or racoon scuttle across the property and cause the sensors to kick in. She looked down again as the light went out. With a long wooden spoon she stirred the mush around, grimacing. On any other day it would have been fine but now it just looked like wallpaper paste and smelled like cat food. Sara groaned and banged the spoon on the edge of the pot.

Leaving it on the counter to cool she crossed to the phone and picked it up. Still no dial tone. Of course this was reality for everyone in the country barring the few who had the old-style ones not powered by AC, but hers should have been working, at least for longer than a few days. Outside the generator chugged steadily then spluttered a little.

While waiting for Max, she slipped into her dark jacket and lined winter boots and flung a brown scarf around her face preparing to go out and check that it had enough gas for the next few hours. Hank said he'd left some additional gasoline in the shed. A wall of cold hit her, piercing her body as she braved the snow and made her way over to the generator. She shut it off and unscrewed the top before collecting the canister of gasoline and refilling it. As it splashed into the generator she glanced out of the shed down the driveway. The sensor had kicked on again and illuminated the yard. She squinted. Were her eyes deceiving her? Was that Hank's vehicle with the headlights on? She'd seen him leave and drive away. What did he want now? She groaned. That man couldn't take no for an answer.

Sara stopped pouring, screwed the lid back on the generator and made her way out. She cupped a hand over her eyes to block the large snowflakes. "Hank?"

She called out but got no answer. Trudging through the deep snow she made her way down to the truck, grumbling under her breath. She wouldn't have put it past him to go and check on her mother and see if she was telling the truth; that would have been just like him. But even if he had, he wouldn't have got inside, so why was he back?

The engine purred; the headlights were facing the house. She squinted again and could just make out his silhouette inside the vehicle.

"Hank. You know Rita is probably worried sick about you. You really should—"

Momentarily blinded by the glare of the lights she reached out for the door handle, thinking his tires were stuck in the snow. As she pulled the door open, his body slumped out, falling on top of her, taking her down to the ground. Her eyes widened in terror at the sight of blood. His throat had been slit. She screamed and scrambled out from beneath him, backing away; her eyes scanning the terrain. A cold shot of fear ran through her. She slipped as she tried to get to her feet and hurry back to the house. She wasn't five yards from the doorway when the lights of the vehicle went out. She didn't dare look back. Sara burst into the house, slamming the door and locking it behind her. Her thoughts shot past her like vehicles on a busy highway.

The inn had entrances at the front, the side and the rear. She bolted through the house. "Max! Get down here now!" Her voice carried the urgency she felt. Making it to the front, she was grateful to see the door was locked. She almost slipped on a runner rug as she sprinted through the maze of halls to the rear. At the rear, where guests would often retreat to a heavily windowed lounge that overlooked a hilly forested landscape, she noticed the doors were slightly ajar. Crossing to the fireplace she grabbed an iron poker and gripped it with both hands preparing to fight for her life if need be. She scanned the dark room that was only lit by moonlight and hurried to close the doors.

Sara backed away from the closed doors. There was no one outside that she could see but someone had killed Hank. Who? And why? Castine was a sleepy town that catered to tourists; they rarely had to call county police. *The police!* Sara turned and raced toward the kitchen when she slammed into — Max?

She gripped his arms. "You okay?"

"I'm okay, what's the matter with you?"

She rushed past him telling him to stay close.

"Mom, what's the matter?"

"I need you to stay away from the windows. Don't go near the doors."

"Why? Mom, you're freaking me out."

She wasn't paying attention to him. Sara was working off instincts. She snatched up the phone and cried out upon remembering it was dead. Her mind wasn't working right. She should have remembered that but she was juggling multiple thoughts. "Shit!" she said dropping the phone. "The rifle."

Max looked thoroughly disturbed as Sara rushed down the hallway, darted into an office that belonged to Landon and proceeded to unlock the door on the gun cabinet. She pulled out a rifle, snatched up a box of bullets and then dropped them. They scattered across the floor. "Damn it!"

Max darted in to help her. "Mom, would you please just tell me what is going on?"

"Just go up to your room, get in the closet and stay quiet."

"I'm not doing that."

"Max!"

He stared back at her. She was never one to raise her voice so it must have caught him off guard. He backed out of the room while she loaded the rifle. She'd never fired one before but she'd seen Landon load and shoot at targets in the yard multiple times. When he wasn't flying planes he enjoyed going to a local firing range. He said he wanted to do it so he could tag along with a friend of his, who was big into hunting, but she always thought that was just a joke. He hated the wilderness. Too many bugs. One time they'd gone camping in a tent and that ended with them leaving in the middle of the night because he was sure there was an insect biting his leg. It made her laugh. He was a strong man who often flew crappy old planes long distances and didn't bat an eye but throw him into the wilderness and he was like a fish out of water. Then again, so was she.

Sara fumbled with the bullets as she loaded them into the magazine. It could hold up to five rounds. What was it he said? Landon had tried to explain how to use the Thompson Center Compass .270 Winchester. "That's it. That's it," she mumbled. "Open the bolt, keep your finger on the outside of the trigger and inspect the bore for obstructions." She went through it in her head while continuing to look up and listen for anyone in the house besides her and Max. Nothing. It was silent barring the ticking of a clock.

"Mom, who are those people outside?"

"What?" she replied.

She came bounding out thinking he was upstairs only to find him in the kitchen staring out the window. "What did I tell you?" she said.

"But…" He pointed.

Sara looked out. The sensor had kicked in again. In front of the truck were three people. She squinted. They looked familiar. Then it dawned on her. They were the same ones that had attempted to break into Jake's Scout. One of them was holding a baseball bat, another a large knife, and the third what appeared to be a hammer. "Max. Listen to me very carefully." She scooped up a large kitchen knife and handed it to him. "Take this, and go upstairs. No matter what you hear. You don't come down. You understand?"

"I'm not leaving you down here."

"I'll be fine."

"No."

She lifted a hand. "Max!"

Reluctantly he nodded and bolted up the stairs.

Sara took a deep breath, steadied herself and approached the side door. She stepped out, snow falling on her face as she raised the rifle. "This is private property. You are trespassing. I've already called the cops..." She wasn't sure why she said it. Maybe in some grand hope that they were ignorant of what was or wasn't working under the circumstances. Before she could say any more, they immediately fanned out disappearing out of view. The lights went out. A blanket of darkness swallowed everything in sight. She backed off heading into the house when suddenly the generator turned off. She spun around, rifle aimed towards the shed. There was movement. She squeezed the trigger then felt the kickback. Panic rising in her chest, she backed into the house, now there were no lights on at all. She shut the door and backed off into the darkness, scanning the windows as her eyes adjusted to her new world of terror.

From the back of the house, she heard a door rattle as if someone was trying to get in. Moving quickly she hurried to the rear only to find the common room empty.

Then, the sound of glass shattering came from the kitchen.

Her heart was pounding in her chest as she raced to the front of the house to find the window above the lock on the door was broken and the door was now ajar. She backed up only to bump into the kitchen table. Startled, she squeezed the trigger and a round fired into the ceiling. Now in full panic mode she headed for the staircase only to be cut off by a female wearing a hood over her head. She tossed the hammer from hand to hand, her head slightly low, her features indistinguishable.

Sara lifted the rifle just as the woman darted into a different room.

"Why are you doing this?" she bellowed but got no answer.

Moving fast, she crossed the short space between where she was and the staircase. She only made it four steps up when she felt a hard strike to her back. Sara screamed in agony and collapsed, the rifle dropped and slid down to the foot of the staircase where the woman picked up her hammer again. Sara glanced at the rifle, as did the woman. Why didn't she grab it? If she wanted to kill her, a bullet would be quicker. But maybe they didn't want them to die quick. Groaning in pain, Sara gripped her back and ascended while the woman watched her. She didn't chase her. It was as if she was enjoying the fear.

Sara blasted into Max's room and closed the door.

There was no lock. Nothing to protect them. She could have told him to hide in one of the bathrooms but only a few had windows, and those were tiny, certainly not enough to offer a way out. Besides, locking themselves in one place with no way out seemed like a dumb idea. There were fourteen guest rooms, and three additional rooms for her family, spread out over three floors.

"Mom," Max said rushing over from across the room. He wasn't even in his closet. She couldn't believe it. He was wielding a baseball bat like an axe in one hand and had the knife in the other. She took the knife and told him to get back into the closet while she went over to the window. "Who are they?"

"I don't know." She stumbled over her words. "I saw them outside the grocery store. They were trying to break into Jake's truck."

Max looked confused.

"Hank is dead."

"What?"

"I found him in his vehicle at the end of the driveway. Listen, there is no time to discuss this now, we need to get out of here. I thought I could keep them out but—"

Before she could finish, they heard the sound of someone whistling in a creepy fashion followed by something sharp being dragged over a hard surface. At the window, Sara looked out and saw one of them looking around. *Shit. Think. Think.* She paced for a moment trying to make a decision. If they stayed where they were, they'd eventually be found, then again, she couldn't go out, not with one of them outside.

Max came up alongside her.

"I can go and get help from one of the neighbors."

"No. I can't let you do that."

"Mom."

She shook her head.

"I can do it," he said. "For once trust me."

"I do," she said, turning towards him and looking him

in the eye. She looked out again and saw the guy was gone. "Okay, listen to me. As soon as you get down, hurry over to the Millers'. Don't stop for a second. No matter what you hear."

He nodded and slipped into a warm winter jacket, gripping the bat tightly.

Sara could hear the intruders making their way around the rooms on the floor below. Carefully, Sara shifted up the window and stuck her head out to get a better look. The roof was covered in snow. She grimaced. "I can do it," Max said, reassuring her. Seventeen and yet he had all the courage of an adult. Max stuck a leg out the window, bent at the waist and crawled out. As soon as he was out, she watched him slide down at a crouch to the edge of the roof then drop over onto the next roof. Before she could make sure he'd landed safely, she heard footsteps coming down the hallway, getting closer.

Chapter 25

It was a low crunching sound — too heavy for a cougar or wolf and yet not loud enough to be a bear. Beth stopped what she was doing and cocked her head. It was hard to mistake the presence of another with the silence of the mountain. In years gone by a few hikers had stumbled across their property nestled in the forest, high up in the Blue Ridge Mountains. It wasn't common as the cabin was off the beaten path and most stuck to the trails, however, it did occur. Her father had been quick to make it clear they were trespassing and that was all that needed to be said. Hikers weren't out to cause trouble, most continued on their way unless they were lost but that had only occurred twice. Still, with the way the weather had been over the past few days, it didn't make sense that anyone would be nearby.

The crunching stopped.

Beth turned to reach for a tool under the workbench

when voices followed.

She couldn't make out what they were saying but they were close, far too close to be hikers walking nearby. Beth bolted over to the door and peered through the slatted wood.

Four.

Four flashlight beams brushed the ground, cutting into the darkness and playing off the tree trunks and underbrush as strangers made their way through the last patch of woodland that hedged in the property. Her mind went blank. Had Dr. Banks gone for help? He'd tried to convince her to go with him and that he would return at a later date with further help to get Landon down the mountain. She thanked him but declined. He said it wasn't safe to stay with Landon and that after learning about Rhett, she was in no state to be caring for anyone. She almost agreed. But what would her father have done? And could Landon get better treatment in town where the power was out? It seemed like a waste of resources and manpower, she thought. Instead, she told the doctor that she would monitor him. Once he was strong enough to walk, she would bring him to town.

Again, she wasn't sure what her hesitation was with returning to town, perhaps an unwillingness to leave the cabin, the only anchor to her father, to her past, to who she was. Home meant everything.

With her bow in hand, Beth ambled out of the old shed and made her way to the front of the cabin just as four adults emerged from the tree line. Noting three of them were armed, she knew going for the handgun on her hip wouldn't be a smart move. Common sense trumped speed. She would have been dead before she'd even pulled it. Instead, she waited to see what they wanted.

Her eyes scanned them: a Chinese guy, a bald dude scowling, the next one she'd seen driving around town, average looking, shifty eyes, out of place with a goatee. The fourth guy was taller and looked like military with light tactical pants, a form-fitting parka and a dark beanie that framed his heavily bearded face.

"Well, hello there," the bearded guy said, raising a

hand and stopping twenty yards away. He casually thumbed over his shoulder. "The plane that crashed. We were told you have the survivor. That right?"

Beth didn't answer.

The man looked at one of the others then back at her. When he did, he smiled and motioned to the rifles. "Oh, the guns? That's just for protection. We ran into a cougar on the way up. Listen, Dr. Banks told us he was here. We figured we could bring him to town where he can get real medical treatment. Okay?"

One of the guys stepped forward heading for the cabin and in an instant, she had an arrow on that bow and ready to fire. Guns were raised but the bearded guy told them to lower their weapons. Shifty Eyes stopped in his tracks and stared at her. He might have had a rifle in hand but there was fear in his eyes.

The bearded fella took a few steps forward with his hand out trying to control the situation. "Whoa. It's okay. We're not here to harm you."

"He's staying," Beth replied confidently. "Now leave."

There was a long pause. The man seemed to be amused or taken aback by her courage. "Well... I'm afraid I can't do that. You see, there was something on that plane that belongs to me. Now we checked and it's not there. So I was hoping that maybe you found it? Or perhaps the man you're looking after knows where it is. So how about you put that bow down before you get injured," he said, strongly emphasizing it would be her not them on the receiving end of pain.

Beth began taking small steps back towards the door. If she could get inside, she could increase the odds of survival. She wanted to live but after losing her parents she was in a dark place, and more than willing to die on that mountain if need be.

"Just give us the bag, kid, and we'll be on our way."

She said nothing but kept moving.

"You're getting the bag... right?" he asked, nodding as if that would somehow persuade her. Was he stupid? The contents meant nothing to her. She had no qualms about handing it over if it meant they could live but she wasn't foolish. Beth knew anyone associated with that bag was as good as dead.

"Oh fuck this!" the bald-headed one said. He raised his gun and Beth had no choice but to fire the arrow, it flew through the air and embedded in the top of his thigh sending him down. Before they had a chance to react, the back of her boot struck the door and she quickly reached for the handle and backed inside.

Chapter 26

Max's bedroom was closing in on Sara. She clamped her hand tightly around the knife and crouched in the darkness, afraid to move out of fear of being heard. Outside, in the hallway, she could hear one of them tearing a room apart searching for her.

If it was food they wanted, why not just take it and leave? Or was this payback?

She heard boots on the hardwood floor in the room next door and knew that if she didn't make a break for it now, Max's room was next. If she could reach the stairs, she could collect the rifle and flee through the kitchen. Sara opened the bedroom door and took a quick glance. No movement. They were in Ellie's room. Sara darted out into the bathroom across from her. She tucked herself behind the door in a way so she could see through the thin crack of the door and frame.

A figure loomed into view, hammer in hand.

Her heartbeat raced as she tried not to breathe.

It was the woman. She entered Max's room and disappeared into the darkness. Some part of her wanted to stay still, avoid detection. Self-preservation had kicked into high gear and fear made her feet feel like lead. *Go. Go now!* A stronger voice told her.

She waited for activity in her son's room before budging; anything that would mask her movement. Sara slipped out and took a few steps. Her eyes darted to his room. Every step was slow and controlled, not wanting to attract attention. Had the house not been so old she might have made it to the staircase.

Creak.

The floorboard groaned beneath her.

A wave of anxiety. Sara looked back and saw the woman dart out.

Both of them made a beeline for the stairs. She took the first five almost in one leap, slamming her shoulder into the wall before the woman threw the hammer.

Five inches

That was all it missed by.

Sara took off down the next steps with the woman hot on her trail.

* * *

It was freezing outside. Max had waited on the lower roof until he was sure he couldn't hear anyone before plunging into a snowdrift that had formed against the house. His stomach caught in his throat as fear got the better of him. His limbs cramped as he struggled to get up. He'd played all manner of violent and scary video games but nothing came close to this. Baseball bat in one hand, he swatted snow out of his eyes as he crawled out of the ice tomb.

There were three homes nearby, one to the north that required cutting through a grove of trees, and the other two were across the street. The challenge was reaching them. The inn's grounds were vast, and with so much snow on the ground he had to work that much harder to wade through it.

Still, determined, Max clenched his jaw and moved

out.

All the while he kept looking over his shoulder, worried more for his mother than himself. *I should have stayed,* he told himself. But his mother was stubborn. A huge gust of wind kicked up ice needles in his face nearly taking his breath away. A wall of snow before him blinded his view of the Millers' property. It was a modest home just off Woodside Way. They were close friends of the family. Tom Miller was in his late sixties, a carpenter by trade. His wife, Julie, had owned an antique store in town. Both retired early and now spent most of their days working in the yard. Julie was a bit of a horticulturist and loved to be out there at the crack of dawn working in the flower bed while Tom was often found in his garage creating cedar chairs that he would sell out the front of their home. In the summers, when they were younger, Max and his sister would often take over baked goods that their mother had made.

As soon as he arrived on the Millers' property, he called out to them but got no answer. He hurried to the back of their home and tried the door but it was locked. All the while he looked over his shoulder expecting someone to attack at any second. Max dashed around to the front to find the door open.

"Tom. Julie? It's Max."

He used the tip of the baseball bat to push it wide. Snow footprints led in and out. Had they left and forgot to lock the door? No. Tom was OCD and would have checked it three times. Max called out to them again and ventured in if only to check that they were okay. It was a simple layout. A living room in the rear, a kitchen and dining area to the right, and stairs that went up to a second floor with two bedrooms and a bathroom.

Max made it into the living room. He squinted into the dark trying to reach the curtains which were drawn. He opened them partially to let some of the moon's light filter in. That's when he saw a pair of feet sticking out from behind the couch. He backed up only to trip over something and land hard, his hand sinking into wetness. Gasping in the grip of fear, he smelled the scent of iron and saw Julie lying in a puddle of blood. Max scrambled to his feet, rushing back to the hallway to leave only to find his exit blocked by a large figure holding a steel baseball bat.

Max raised his bat, shaking it in front of him in a threatening way. "Stay back. Stay back." The hooded figure ambled through the open doorway without any hesitation. "I'm warning you."

Then, it happened.

The figure charged forward; the bat extended out like a battering ram. Max swung his and steel connected with steel, clattering loudly, once, twice, three times as they swung the bats at each other. Max ducked, coming dangerously close to having his head taken off. He burst forward, slamming into the stranger, knocking him over the couch and landing on top of Tom's lifeless body.

In a band of moonlight he could see his attacker's face.

He didn't recognize him, it was just a guy, late twenties.

In a fight for his life, Max rolled off him and tried to

flee. He didn't make it.

The guy grabbed his ankle and he crashed into a table breaking it in two. The guy was on him so fast he didn't have time to catch his breath. The guy pulled his baseball bat over Max's head and dug it deep into his throat. An arm of steel forced against his neck; a knee jammed into the small of his back. Max managed to slip his fingers around the bat but the guy was strong. He knew if he didn't change position, and fast, he'd pass out. Fingers raked at the bat, his attacker said nothing. He could hear him grunting as he wrenched on the bat trying to end Max's life.

He reached one hand back and dug his fingers into his pocket trying to pull out a set of keys to the house. Gasping for breath he could feel his throat closing in on him. Suddenly, his hands clasped the keys and he pushed one between his fingers and yanked them out. Using the key like a knife, and holding it tight in his hand, he used every ounce of strength to twist over onto his back. The madman above him just saw that as an opportunity to press the bat down on his neck. He must have thought Max was making it easier for him. He wasn't.

As soon as he saw the opening, Max reached up and stuck the end of the key into the side of the guy's throat, not once, or even twice but multiple times in a frenzied attack.

His attacker slumped on top of him bleeding out and covering him in blood.

Pale from shock, Max forced him off and didn't stick around to fish through his pocket to see who he was. It didn't matter. Not now. He bolted out of the door and was about to head to the home of the next neighbor when he heard glass smash at the inn, followed by a scream.

"Mom!"

Chapter 27

Beth thought fast. She'd opened a Pandora's box and there was no going back now. What little hope they had was gone. "Beth? Who's out there?" Landon asked her as she hurried over to the rifle and scooped it up but not before taking the handgun from her holster and handing it to him. Grizzly bounded around her, stopping occasionally to growl and bark at the door.

"Death," she replied.

"What?" He glanced at the handgun. "Beth, what is going on?"

Beth gathered up the brick of cocaine she'd thrown at Landon and stuffed it back in the bag then lugged it over to the door. She peeked outside and saw them dragging the guy she'd shot in the leg back to the tree line.

"Men," she bellowed. "Four of them. The same ones you probably work for. They want this," she said pointing to the bag.

"So give it to them."

"It's too late," she said making sure there was a round chambered in the rifle. She brought it up and stood at an angle near the window to get a better lay of the land. With darkness upon them but the moon lighting up the clearing, she was able to distinguish where they were.

"Beth. Listen to me."

"I shot one in the leg."

Landon shook his head in disbelief. "You did what?"

"He was about to kill me," she said in defense before squinting out at the forest. Landon flung his cover off and tried to get up but it was impossible. Both legs were splinted and cast. He wasn't going anywhere.

"You need to stay put," she said. "I'll handle this."

"Handle this? You're a child."

"Seventeen nearly eighteen. Hardly a child."

"No. No, Beth, I'll talk with them. I'm older than you, they'll..."

"Understand?" She cut him off, then chuckled shaking her head. She knew, although he was older than her, that she was the one with experience, with knowledge of these woods. If her father had taught her anything about living off the grid, it was that at the basic primal level, all of wildlife knew that in order to survive you had to be willing to kill. It wasn't personal, it was survival. "These men don't understand. Do you think they understood my mother?" She glanced at him. "No, they'll kill both of us. The only way out of here now is to kill them first."

"Kill? What!" Landon took a deep breath. "Okay, Beth. Put the gun down and…"

"Grizzly, come here, boy." She ignored him and got down and whispered into the dog's ear. When she got up the dog scampered off into the adjoining room and returned a moment later with her bag. She slipped it onto her back and gave the dog instructions to stay and protect Landon. From there she crossed into the dining area and shifted the table back across the wooden floor, then flipped back a large area rug to reveal a round iron handle. Beth looked at Landon. "They come through that door. Shoot. Don't hesitate. Shoot. Grizzly will protect you but don't rely on him. I'll do what I can," she said lifting the floor door.

"Beth. Wait," Landon said but she didn't. She dropped down into darkness and closed the door above her. Her father hadn't built the cabin with survival in mind, so to speak, but practicality. The area beneath the cabin was meant to be used like a pantry, a cold storage room for additional supplies like grain, dried and canned goods, but it also offered a second way out. She could have dragged Landon into it but she figured he'd stand a better chance holding them back from inside the cabin while she ducked into the woods and circled around to take them out.

In her mind this was no different than hunting feral boars. It was dangerous but necessary. The damn things wreaked havoc on the land and were a hugely destructive species.

Beneath the cabin there was about four feet of space, she had to crouch and shuffle along to the rear where she pulled back a section of wood that took her into an exposed area beneath the cabin. Beyond that a trellis and wire meshing went around the opening to prevent animals from getting in. She could hear one of the men cursing, and another in agony. Thank you, she said under her breath, grateful for them giving away their location. She'd never killed anyone but after all she'd been through, what she'd witnessed her mother go through and under the circumstances she was ready to cross that line.

Beth pulled back the wire meshing, then kicked out the trellis until she was able to crawl out and slide down a steep embankment at the rear. Her clothes were drenched but her mind pushed out the feelings of cold. Blasting away from the cabin, fear drove her on as her legs pounded the earth beneath her. She had a small advantage, the element of surprise, and she intended to capitalize on it. Darkness and dense woodland were her friends as she circled around the group.

She could hear them arguing about what to do.

Two of them wanted to head into the cabin, the other was against it.

"We have no idea what we're going into."

"I don't give a fuck. That bitch put an arrow in me."

"Morgan, calm down. I need to think."

"Why don't we just set the cabin on fire?"

"Tommy. Are you an idiot? My gear is in that cabin."

"Cayden, look. She's just a girl."

"And her old man was just a guy but he got in the way."

Beth stopped moving, shock setting in. Was that an admission to her father's death? "Yeah, what was the deal with that? The lights were out. It's not like the cops were gonna do anything."

"It only takes one fly in the ointment to screw it up. He was a liability. A man like that doesn't walk away and say nothing." As Beth listened, she couldn't believe her ears. What had her father got involved in? And why had he hidden it from her? She was beginning to think she never really knew her parents. Anger turned to fury and she brought up her arrow and scrambled forward preparing to unleash hell.

Chapter 28

Quit. It wasn't in Sara's vocabulary. If her mother had taught her anything, it was cry if you must — wallow in self-pity for a moment — but eventually pick yourself up, brush yourself off and press on. And yet in that moment all she wanted to do was lay there and die.

Minutes earlier she'd reached the bottom of the stairs only to find the rifle gone.

Hearing the woman chasing her, she'd darted into the kitchen hoping to make it out the door only to be cut off by the second attacker. She'd hurled a plant on the table at him before sprinting back to the living room only to find the handles on the patio doors had been locked.

With no time to waste she tossed a chair at the window, figuring she could crawl out. That escape attempt had failed miserably. No sooner had she begun to climb out than she was yanked back in by her hair. She slid across the hardwood and slammed into the wall. The woman switched hands on the hammer and shoved a small table out of the way as she charged over ready to unleash one hell of a beating.

As she brought the hammer down, Sara lunged forward and drove the blade into the woman's rib cage thinking it would stop her but it didn't, it only made her lash out with more intensity, cracking her in the side of the face with the hammer.

Sara blacked out.

It was hard to know how long she was unconscious but it couldn't have been long as when she awoke the woman was lying on the ground nearby, coughing and staring at her; gripping the knife that was still deep in her rib cage.

Seconds elapsed. From across the room she heard a thunderous pounding of boots as someone hurried over then stopped abruptly. A groan of anguish. With blood dripping down her forehead blurring her vision, Sara peered through pain at the attacker. He pushed back his hood and dropped to a crouch beside the woman, cupping a hand around her face. Sara heard him telling her to hang in there, then he flashed her an angry sideways glance. *Shit.*

He gritted his teeth and came at her, all spit and fury with the knife raised.

This was it.

This was where it would end.

There was no more fight left in her. She wasn't a quitter but she couldn't lie to herself either. She attempted to get up but her vision went sideways until the man was nothing more than a red blur.

She squeezed her eyes tight waiting for the inevitable and the piercing pain of a knife but it never came. A sudden metallic thud, then another and another followed. Opening her eyes, she saw the man was lying face down with Max hunched on top of him, beating him in the head with his baseball bat.

"Max. Stop," she said but he either didn't hear her or was gripped by so much fear that he couldn't even if he wanted to. She clawed at the hardwood floor trying to make her way over and that was when he saw her. His hands were shaking. Max dropped the bat and fell to his knees.

"Mom," he said staring at his bloody hands.

"It's okay. I'm here."

She reached him and wrapped an arm around his waist and he wiped blood from her forehead. "The other?" she asked.

"Dead."

Sara looked over at the woman. She was no longer breathing.

They remained there for another five minutes before they got up and Max helped her out of the house down to Hank's truck. The keys were still in the ignition and the engine idling. "I'll drive," Max said.

* * *

Fifteen minutes later they arrived outside Jake's home on the east side of town. Max helped his mother out of the vehicle, his arm gripped her waist while her arm hung loosely over his shoulder. He carried her up to the front door, calling out to Jake, but his voice was lost in the howling wind. She kept going in and out of consciousness on the way over. "Mom. We're here." She mumbled something as he banged hard on the door. A few minutes then the door cracked wide.

"Max? Sara!" Jake rushed out and helped her into the house.

Max turned and looked out before closing the door. A trail of blood in the glistening snow marked the path they'd taken, and foretold the challenges to come.

Chapter 29

Under the cover of woods, Beth watched the four men fan out around the cabin. Using her rifle made sense but it also would give away her location and with the odds stacked against her, remaining out of sight was all she had working for her.

That and her knowledge of the terrain.

Taking out four adults had less to do with age or skill and more to do with opportunity. It was all about timing. She was comfortable in her environment, they weren't. She removed the bow and laid it down in the underbrush while she slung the rifle strap over her head and scooped it behind her back.

The plan was to take them out one by one.

If she could do that silently, even better.

Next, she climbed up into a big oak tree, straddled a large branch and focused her attention on the Chinese guy, who was the closest. Taking an arrow and laying it across the bow, she pulled back and slowed her breathing. *One shot. That might be all you get.* Even using a bow she wouldn't be able to stay hidden. They would hunt her down but at least if she could draw them away from the cabin it might offer Landon a better chance of survival. She knew these woods like the back of her hand, it would be like leading them into a maze where only she knew the route to take.

The Chinese guy was crouched near a tree, his AR-15 aimed directly at one of the cabin windows. Hitting him through the heart would be the easiest shot but there was a chance he wouldn't die immediately and his cries would attract the others. No, she aimed for the back of his neck, it would cut off his windpipe and possibly…

Before she could finish the thought, they opened fire on the cabin peppering it with as many rounds as possible from different angles. Muzzle flashes lit up the night as glass shattered, wood spat and holes appeared in the structure.

Beth released the arrow.

It was a perfect shot. The Chinese guy slumped forward without letting out even a whimper. Under the noise of gunfire the other three didn't even notice as she scaled down the tree and shifted position, withdrawing another arrow. One down, three to go.

The assault on the cabin ceased and she stopped running and hunkered down behind a large trunk, then moved up behind a boulder.

"Tommy!"

Damn it! They'd spotted him.

Beth caught movement.

"She's out here. I told you. We should have killed her when we had the chance," the bald guy said. All eyes were now on the forest, scanning, trying to pinpoint her location. She held her breath not wanting to release even a wisp of air.

The bearded fellow they referred to as Cayden dropped to a crouch and directed Shifty Eyes over to his left while he went right. Baldy didn't keep his position, instead he turned towards the cabin. *No.* She couldn't let that happen.

Pulling back an arrow, she fired again, this time however because he was moving it struck him in the shoulder. He let out a cry and cursed loudly before snapping it and continuing towards the door. "Over there!" Baldy bellowed figuring out her rough location based on where the arrow had hit him.

Beth blasted away from the boulder as rounds tore up soil, tree trunks and rock around her. The hunt was on.

* * *

Lying on the ground, his arm holding Grizzly down, Landon felt another wave of pain ripple up his legs. The rapid succession of gunfire tearing up the cabin gave him no other choice than to roll off the bed and stay low. The sudden impact of the drop felt almost as bad as the first time he tried to move inside the plane. A series of terrifying thoughts came to him: What if Beth was dead or worse — injured? What if they burst in and tortured him before putting him out of his misery?

He thought back to Beth's warning. If they enter,

shoot, don't hesitate. He'd been to a firing range, unloaded more than his fair share of rounds at paper targets, but killing a human? Could he really do that?

Grizzly growled and struggled within his grasp. "Whoa, boy, sit still," he said but it was useless, Grizzly was staring at the door barking loudly and Landon was losing his grip on the collar. The sound of boots outside, and a rattle of the door followed by multiple rounds fired at the lock, and he knew why the dog was losing it.

He released his grip just as the door burst open.

The man managed to get one leg in the door before Grizzly broke away from Landon at a full sprint and leaped in the air taking the man outside. The door slammed shut and he could hear the dog going crazy. "Grizzly!" he yelled. Unable to move his legs and with the P320 in hand, Landon clawed towards the door with his other arm.

A sudden round and a high-pitched howl from the dog marked the end of the commotion outside. *No. No!* He brought up the handgun preparing for the worst.

Outside he heard cursing then the door was kicked open.

Landon rolled behind the table, brought the gun up and held it with both hands as a man staggered into view and unleashed a flurry of rounds, all of which were squeezed off at hip level. He spotted his opportunity and fired the gun, once, twice.

The bullets went into his thigh and knee.

The guy dropped; his rifle slid across the smooth wooden floor.

As the man gripped his leg in agony, cursing and screaming, Landon rolled into view to take another shot only to have a knife thrown at him. It hit him in the upper right shoulder. Before he had a chance to fire a round, the guy dragged himself behind a wall that divided his room from the rest of the cabin. Still, Landon squeezed off five rounds through the wooden wall, hoping for a lucky shot.

No such luck.

He heard the man laugh. "I'm gonna gut you like a

pig."

Landon winced as he reached up and pulled the knife from his shoulder and scrambled back against the bed, waiting for the man to emerge. He could hear him moving, crying out in pain but trying to do something. What was he up to? Landon held out the gun knowing he had ten rounds left. He unleashed another four at the wall hoping to catch him. One of them hit its mark as he heard the man wail. "You mother—"

"Is she alive?" Landon asked cutting him off. There was a pause.

"Not for long," the guy replied.

Chapter 30

Beth's throat burned as she raced through the blackness of the forest using what little night sight she had. A crescent moon loomed overhead offering minuscule rays of light that pierced through a canopy of coniferous spruce-fir. The sky was unusually dark that night with no stars visible.

With snow falling and limited vision, trees came into view only when they were a few feet away. She threaded her way around, sidestepping and lunging over large roots as she tried to avoid the onslaught of rounds lancing trees. Cold, with adrenaline pumping through her system, she barely noticed branches slapping her in the face or pain in her ankles as she tried to remain upright over uneven ground.

Slipping her bow over her shoulder, she brought the rifle around and crouched by a tree, listening to where the men were. "She went that way!"

"No, I've got tracks here. Russ…"

She squinted through a flurry of snow and saw Cayden giving Russ directions.

Would they give up if she kept on running? She doubted it. They would just double back and finish Landon and… Grizzly. She felt a twinge of pain at hearing her dog yelp. If they killed him, she'd go berserk. That was her only family now.

Her father's voice came back to her in that moment like a lost memory.

They'd been out hunting, trying to locate wild boar, and fear had got the better of her after several close encounters. Though boar were more inclined to run from humans, attacks did happen. They were vicious and depending on who you asked, they were known to be even more dangerous than bears. She'd heard stories from her father of them killing a local man who was trying to protect his dogs.

I know you're scared but just breathe. You can do this.

And like that she was back in the moment.

Beth watched as Cayden went off to her left and Shifty Eyes disappeared out of view. *Where did you go?*

She wanted to scale a tree to get a better lay of the land but any sudden movement was liable to give away her position. Carefully stepping out from behind a boulder she darted across to a tree and scanned her field of vision. Nothing.

Then movement.

Beth spun around but wasn't fast enough.

A gun butt struck her in the face and she found herself on the ground, her rifle gone. Scrambling, she raked the ground around her.

"Forget it. Go now before he finds you."

She looked up to find Shifty Eyes holding her rifle and jerking his head towards the forest. "I'll tell him you got away."

"Why?"

"It doesn't matter. Just go."

"Did you kill my father Rhett?"

He stared at her, cast a glance over his shoulder then

took a few steps back. "Kid, you don't want to get involved in this. Go now."

"Did you?" she asked. She had to know.

"No. Cayden did. Now get the fuck out of here before I change my mind."

She could see he was torn but why was he letting her go? She began to scramble when the other man emerged from the forest. His eyes darted between her and Shifty Eyes. "Russ. What the fuck…?" And like that he lifted his gun and went to fire a round at her but Russ lunged at him knocking the gun down. The revolver went off and a round tore up the earth nearby. Beth bounced up and pulled an arrow in an attempt to kill Cayden but the two of them were now rolling on the ground, down the slope, through the snow. She tried to get a bead on him but it was impossible without risking killing the other guy.

More rounds erupted from the cabin.

She looked that way and then back at the men.

Stay or go back?

The decision was purely selfish, a desire to kill the man

who'd murdered her father. The same group that was responsible for the death of her mother, a death that was filed away by cops as nothing more than an overdose but she knew the truth. At least the truth according to her father, now even that she doubted.

Turning back, she watched as the two men rolled over a bluff and vanished.

For a second there was no sound, and then one single shot echoed.

Beth pitched sideways and with her bow in one hand and the other gripping branches, she made her way to the edge of the bluff and peered over. The two of them were lying motionless. Were they dead? She hurried around and down a trail that opened up near where the men were. As she came around a large beech tree, only one man was in the snow — Russ. Her eyes scanned to the left, then right. *Where are you?*

She backed up only to feel the brunt force of something hard against her head.

It didn't knock her out but it dropped her.

"Just like your old man. Always getting in the way."

Cayden lumbered into view, limping.

"Why?" she asked.

"It's not personal, kid, just business. Your mother? That was personal."

Rage welled up inside her, her hand sliding to the machete on her hip. Cayden noticed. "You've got courage, kid; I give you that. But now…"

He raised his revolver and cocked it. She didn't close her eyes but went for the machete. She didn't stand a chance but if she was gonna die, she would die fighting.

A round cracked.

She turned her head and saw Russ drop his rifle.

Cayden gripped his chest and his knees buckled and he fell face first into the snow.

Beth sat there for a second or two, unable to believe it was over. She scrambled back and hurried over to Russ who was gripping his own wound. "Sorry," he managed to say before coughing up blood. His eyes glazed over and he was gone.

* * *

Huddled in the corner of the cabin, Landon waited. Any second now he expected Baldy to emerge, a final assault that would end with one of them dead. He glanced at the handgun. He'd all but used up what rounds were in the magazine, firing randomly at the wall hoping to take him out before he attacked. One round had got him but the rest missed. Would he attack? He'd shot him multiple times. Maybe he was bleeding out behind the wall. There had been no movement for several minutes and for a fleeting moment, he felt a spark of hope that perhaps he was dead.

That hope died as his attacker tossed something out and Landon reacted by firing the last round out of fear. Laughter followed. "I'd say you're out of ammo now," the man said. The bastard had been waiting him out. Expecting him to use up his rounds so he could then waltz out and finish him in brutal fashion. From the edge of the wall he saw the man hold out a small mirror and he caught him smile.

Movement.

Boots scuffing the wood floor.

The man stumbled into view, and Landon gripped the knife with both hands.

"Come on then," he said. "Come on!"

Baldy's lip curled as he yelled and charged forward.

He made it all of three steps before the door burst open and Grizzly attacked. With one leg out of order, Grizzly soon made easy work of him — taking him to the ground and biting at his arms, legs, and then clamping onto his neck. The man fought back punching the dog but Grizzly refused to let go.

Landon clawed his way over to help as Grizzly tore at the man's flesh.

He yelped as Baldy grabbed the dog and tried to toss him but Grizzly just released his grip and picked a different area on the man. By that point, Landon was within reach. He plunged the knife into the man's chest while Baldy focused on trying to get the dog loose.

He cried out in agony and Landon held on for dear life

using his upper body weight to hold the knife in while Grizzly tore at the man until his body went limp.

When he breathed his last, Landon looked over at Grizzly who slumped down and laid on his side breathing heavily. He could make out blood in his fur but couldn't tell if it was his or the man's. Landon was shocked he'd returned to protect him. The door burst open and Beth raced in, her eyes scanning fast. A quick assessment of the situation and she crouched near her dog, placing her hand over a wound. *No. No!* Grizzly raised his head. "Is he okay?" Landon asked.

She shook her head, unsure. "He's hurt bad."

The last thing he saw was her scoop the dog up and take him out of the cabin.

Epilogue

Two months later

The silence of the mountain was remarkable. Landon now understood why Rhett had brought his family into its solitude. It was something he believed Ellie would have loved. The babble of a stream, the rustle of leaves, and fewer snowflakes would mark the end to a brutal winter. The Blue Ridge Mountains that usually attracted hikers from all over the country with its rich and dense forest would soon burst forth with color and life. However, unlike years gone by, hikers wouldn't be found trekking through its well-worn paths, nor indulging in the peace, for the country they had known was no more.

Two months and the power grid was still not up.

For them it meant little as Beth was used to the rhythm of living off the grid, hunting for food and surviving off the land, but for modern humans it was a new world full of challenges and danger.

Landon limped out of the cabin into the bright afternoon sunshine. The earth was covered in a fine layer of snow, a far cry from the winter he'd arrived in. He'd become pretty good at getting around on crutches. The cast on his left leg had been removed a few days earlier but the other one would stay on for the full three months. Though eager to return to Maine, and his family, he knew the journey would be long and treacherous and only made harder if he wasn't healed.

He glanced off to his right and saw Beth in the small graveyard not far from the greenhouse that gave life. The irony of death and life so close together wasn't lost. Landon crutched over to the gated area. Beth was wearing a thick gray winter coat, jeans and dark boots. He had donned one of Rhett's many thick sweaters, a beanie and track pants that Beth had cut to allow room for the cast.

She turned slightly upon hearing him.

There before her were three mounds of earth, with two-foot wooden crosses driven into the ground at the head of them. "Hey," Landon said in a soft voice as he sidled up to her and looked down at the final resting place of her parents, and Ellie.

When she didn't reply he continued. "You okay?"

She nodded and bit down on her lower lip. "My father and I were planning to hike the Appalachian Trail together once I turned eighteen. We'd been talking about it for years." She shook her head and Landon could feel her pain. "Preparing. Collecting gear. Talking about some of the towns we'd stop in along the way. And…" she trailed off, her brow furrowing.

"That's a long way," he said.

"Yeah, about 2,200 miles spread out over fourteen states."

He nodded. "Were you planning on starting nearby?"

She chuckled lost in thought. "I wanted to but my father was a die-hard enthusiast. He said if we didn't start at Springer Mountain in Georgia it wouldn't be real. That's where everyone usually starts if they're heading north."

"Arriving in Katahdin in Maine, right?" he said.

She nodded glancing at him.

"When were you planning on leaving?"

"Probably in March or the first half of April. That would get us there before the park closed." He was familiar with the hike. Anyone who had shown any interest in hiking was. It was famous. People all over the world flocked to do it every year, either heading north or south. It took the average person anywhere from five to seven months to complete it. A few speedsters had managed to do it in less than fifty days but that was without stopping in towns and relied on support from others along the way. It certainly wasn't for the faint of heart. Many unprepared or impatient hikers gave up after a week or two, realizing what they'd got themselves into.

"Castine is about sixty miles from Katahdin. I'm not your father but I'll be heading that way in a month or two," he said looking down at his leg and hoping for a speedy recovery. "Maybe we could go together."

"Together?"

He shrugged. "Look, I know this place is beautiful but with all that's happened in the country, maybe…"

"Thank you, Landon. Really. But this is home," she said turning away. Landon looked at Ellie's grave and nodded before following her over to a bench where she was taking fat off a deer's hide. Grizzly came bounding out of the cabin with a slight limp, wagging his tail. Landon reached down and ruffled the hair on the back of his neck. The dog had taken a liking to him since he'd been there. He wasn't sure if it was because of seeing him every day or because they both shared a similar injury. "Hey boy," he said looking over to Beth who glanced at him. "Amazing what a few months can do, isn't it?" he said with a smile. "He's completely changed his view of me. Don't you think?"

Her lip curled. "He'll miss you when you leave," she replied as she ran the tool back and forth over the deer's hide, then picked off a few pieces of fat and tossed them to Grizzly who swallowed them without chewing.

"He won't if he goes with me."

She pulled a face. "Grizzly stays with me."

"I know."

She squinted then said, "I'm not going with you, Landon, and you can't convince me."

A grin formed. "Of course not. But I still have another month or two to heal. A lot can change, that's all I'm saying. Hey, Grizzly!" he said, then whistled. The dog turned and charged after him, running past him into the cabin. Landon looked back at Beth whose mouth was agape. Landon eyed her. "See, a lot can change,' he said. Beth pursed her lips together, trying hard not to smile as she continued to work away and he crutched back into the cabin.

Landon wasn't prepared to give up or leave without her. There was no telling if time would change her mind, but one thing was sure, he was going home, to Sara, to Max and to the world he'd left behind, or what little still remained.

.

* * *

THANK YOU FOR READING

Book #2 All That Survives is now available. There are four books in this series. Please consider leaving a review. Even a few words is really appreciated. Thanks kindly,

Jack.

A Plea

Thank you for reading All That Remains: A Post-Apocalyptic EMP Survival Thriller (Lone Survivor Series Book 1). If you enjoyed the book, I would really appreciate it if you would consider leaving a review. Without reviews, an author's books are virtually invisible on the retail sites. It also lets me know what you liked. You can leave a review by visiting the book's page. I would greatly appreciate it. It only takes a couple of seconds.

Thank you — **Jack Hunt**

Newsletter

Thank you for buying All That Remains: A Post-Apocalyptic EMP Survival Thriller (Lone Survivor Series book 1), published by Direct Response Publishing.

Click here to receive special offers, bonus content, and news about new Jack Hunt's books. Sign up for the newsletter. http://www.jackhuntbooks.com/signup/

About the Author

Jack Hunt is the author of horror, sci-fi and post-apocalyptic novels. He currently has over thirty books published. Jack lives on the East coast of North America. If you haven't joined Jack Hunt's Private Facebook Group you can request to join by going here. https://www.facebook.com/groups/1620726054688731/ This gives readers a way to chat with Jack, see cover reveals, and stay updated on upcoming releases. There is also his main Facebook page if you want to browse that.

www.jackhuntbooks.com

jhuntauthor@gmail.com

Made in the USA
Coppell, TX
05 February 2020